W9-BWH-093

WITHDRAWN
No longer the property of the
Boston Public Library.
Sale of this material benefits the Library."

DUDLEY BRANCH LIBRARY

SONS OF

The
SCRIBE

a novella

ENCOURAGEMENT

FRANCINE RIVERS

TYNDALE HOUSE PUBLISHERS, INC.
CAROL STREAM, ILLINOIS

DUDLEY BRANCH LIBRARY

*To men of faith who serve
in the shadow of others.*

✦ ✦ ✦

Visit Tyndale's exciting Web site at www.tyndale.com

Check out the latest about Francine Rivers at www.francinerivers.com

TYNDALE and Tyndale's quill logo are registered trademarks of Tyndale House Publishers, Inc.

The Scribe

Copyright © 2007 by Francine Rivers. All rights reserved.

"Seek and Find" section written by Peggy Lynch.

Cover illustration copyright © 2007 by Philip Howe. All rights reserved.

Author photo copyright © 1999 by John Teague. All rights reserved.

Designed by Jennifer Ghionzoli

Edited by Kathryn S. Olson

Scripture quotations are taken from the *Holy Bible*, New Living Translation, copyright © 1996, 2004. Used by permission of Tyndale House Publishers, Inc., Carol Stream, Illinois 60188. All rights reserved.

Library of Congress Cataloging-in-Publication Data

Rivers, Francine, date.
    The scribe / Francine Rivers.
        p. cm. — (Sons of encouragement ; #5)
    ISBN-13: 978-0-8423-8269-4
    ISBN-10: 0-8423-8269-0
    1. Silas (Biblical figure)—Fiction. 2. Bible. O.T.—History of Biblical events—Fiction. 3. Religious fiction. I. Title.
    PS3568.I83165S37 2007
    813'.54—dc22   2007005467

Printed in the United States of America

13   12   11   10   09   08   07
7   6   5   4   3   2   1

acknowledgments

I want to thank my husband, Rick Rivers, for listening to my ideas and challenging and encouraging me through the course of this series. I also want to thank Peggy Lynch, who knew the questions to ask to make me dig deeper into the Scriptures for new insights. I offer special thanks to Kathy Olson for her pruning skills and advice in improving the manuscript. And last, but by no means least, is my gratitude to the entire Tyndale staff for all the work they do in presenting these stories to readers. It's a team effort all the way.

To all of you who have prayed for me over the years and through the course of this particular project, thank you. May the Lord use this story to draw people close to Jesus, our beloved Lord and Savior.

DEAR READER,

This is the last of five novellas on biblical men of faith who served in the shadows of others. These were Eastern men who lived in ancient times, and yet their stories apply to our lives and the difficult issues we face in our world today. They were on the edge. They had courage. They took risks. They did the unexpected. They lived daring lives, and sometimes they made mistakes—big mistakes. These men were not perfect, and yet God in His infinite mercy used them in His perfect plan to reveal Himself to the world.

We live in desperate, troubled times when millions seek answers. These men point the way. The lessons we can learn from them are as applicable today as when they lived thousands of years ago.

These are historical men who actually lived. Their stories, as I have told them, are based on biblical accounts. For the facts we know about the life of Silas, see Acts 15:22 19:10; 2 Corinthians 1:19; 1 Thessalonians 1:1; 2 Thessalonians 1:1; and 1 Peter 5:12.

This book is also a work of historical fiction. The outline of the story is provided by the Bible, and I have started with the information provided for us there. Building on that foundation, I have created action, dialogue, internal motivations, and in some cases, additional characters that I feel are consistent with the biblical record. I have attempted to remain true to the scriptural message in all points, adding only what is necessary to aid in our understanding of that message.

At the end of each novella, we have included a brief study section. The ultimate authority on people of the Bible is the Bible itself. I encourage you to read it for greater understanding. And I pray that as you read the Bible, you will become aware of the continuity, the consistency, and the confirmation of God's plan for the ages—a plan that includes you.

Francine Rivers

SILAS walked to the house where Peter and his wife were
hidden, aggrieved by the weight of the news he bore.

Tapping three times, lightly, he entered the room where
they had often met with brothers and sisters in Christ or
prayed long hours when alone. He found Peter and his
wife in prayer now. Peter's wife raised her head, and her
smile vanished.

Silas helped her up. "We must go," he said softly, and
turned to assist Peter. "Paul has been captured. Soliders
are searching the city for you. You must leave tonight."

As they headed out, Silas explained further. "Apelles
is with me. He will show you the way."

"What about you?" Peter spoke with grave concern.
"You must come with us, Silas. You've served as Paul's secretary as well as mine. They will be looking for you too."

"I'll follow shortly. I was working on a scroll when
Apelles brought me the news. I must return and make certain the ink is dry before I pack it with the others."

Peter nodded gravely, and Silas ducked into the house
where he had been staying. All the papyrus scrolls, except
the one on which he had been working, were already
rolled and stored carefully in leather cases. Silas had
known the day would come when he would have to grab
the pack and run. Lifting the weights that held open the
newest scroll, he rolled the papyrus, and tucked it carefully into its case. As he slung the pack over his shoulder,
he felt the full weight of responsibility to safeguard the
letters.

As he stepped out into the street again, he saw Peter and

his wife and Apelles waiting. Silas ran to them. "Why are you still here?"

Apelles looked frantic. "They wouldn't go farther without you!"

Torn between gratitude for his friends' loyalty and fear for their safety, Silas urged them on. "We must hurry!"

Apelles was clearly relieved to be moving again. He gave further instructions in an urgent whisper. "We have a carriage waiting outside the city gates. We thought it best to wait until nightfall, when the ban on wagons lifted. It will be easier to slip out now."

Peter was well-known in Rome, and would be easily recognized. They would have a better chance of escape in the confusing influx of goods into the city and the cover of darkness beyond the walls.

Peter walked with difficulty, his arm protectively around his wife. "When did the guard come for Paul?"

"They took him to the dungeon this morning." Apelles raised his hand as they came to the end of the street. He peered around the corner and then beckoned them on. The young man made an effort to appear calm, but Silas felt his fear. His own heart beat with foreboding. If captured, Peter would be imprisoned and executed, most likely in some foul spectacle designed by Nero to entertain the Roman mob.

"Silas!" Peter's wife whispered urgently.

Silas glanced back and saw Peter struggling for breath. He caught up to Apelles and grasped his shoulder. "More slowly, my friend, or we'll lose the one we're trying to save."

Peter drew his wife closer and whispered something to her. She held tightly to him and wept into his shoulder.

Peter smiled at Silas. "Right now would be a good time for God to give me wings like an eagle."

Apelles led them more slowly through the dark alleys and narrow streets. Rats fed on refuse as they passed by. The sounds of wagon wheels grew louder. While the city slept, a tide of humanity poured through the gates, bringing with it goods for the insatiable Roman markets. Some drove overladen wagons; others pushed carts. Still others carried heavy packs on their bent backs.

So close to freedom, Silas thought, seeing the open gates just ahead. Could they get through without being recognized?

Apelles drew them close. "Wait here while I make certain it's safe." He disappeared among the wagons and carts.

Silas's heart pounded harder. Sweat trickled down his back. Every minute they stood on the public street added to Peter's danger. He spotted Apelles, his face pale and strained with fear as he struggled through the crowd.

The young man pointed. "That side. Go now! Quickly!"

Silas led the way. His heart lurched when one of the Roman guards turned and looked at him. A Christian brother. Thank God! The Roman nodded once and turned away.

"Now!" Silas made a path for Peter and his wife to pass through the flow. People bumped into them. Someone cursed. A wagon wheel almost crushed Silas's foot.

Once outside the gates and away from the walls, he let Peter set the pace.

An hour down the road, two more friends ran to meet them. "We've been waiting for hours! We thought you'd been arrested!"

Silas took one of them aside. "Peter and his wife are exhausted. Have the coach meet us on the road."

One remained to escort them while the other ran ahead.

When the coach arrived, Silas helped Peter and his wife up and then climbed in with them. Shoulders aching, he shrugged off the heavy pack and leaned back, bracing himself as they set off. The sound of galloping horses soothed his frayed nerves. Peter and his wife were safe—for the moment. The Romans would search the city first, leaving them time to reach Ostia, where the three of them would board the first ship leaving port. Only God knew where they would go next.

Peter looked troubled. His wife took his hand. "What is it, Peter?"

"I don't feel right."

Silas leaned forward, concerned. "Are you ill?" Had the rush through the night been too much for the venerable apostle?

"No, but I must stop."

His wife voiced an objection before Silas could do so. "But, my husband . . ."

Peter looked at Silas.

"As you say." Silas leaned out to signal the coachman.

Peter's wife grabbed him. "Don't, Silas! Please! If they capture Peter, you know what they'll do."

Peter drew her back and put his arm around her. "God has not given us a spirit of fear, my dear, and that's what has sent us racing into darkness."

Silas struck the side of the coach. Leaning out, he called up to the driver to stop. The coach jerked and bounced as it drew to the side of the road. While his wife wept, Peter climbed down. Silas followed. The horses snorted and moved restlessly. Silas shrugged at the driver's questioning look and watched Peter walk off the road.

Peter's wife stepped down. "Go with him, Silas. Reason with him! Please. The church needs him."

Silas walked to the edge of the field and watched over his friend. Why did Peter tarry here?

The old apostle stood in the middle of a moonlit field, praying. Or so Silas thought until Peter paused and tipped his head slightly. How many times over the years had Silas seen Peter do that when someone spoke to him? Silas went closer, and for the barest second something shimmered faintly in the moonlight. Every nerve in his body tingled, aware. Peter was not alone. The Lord was with him.

Peter bowed his head and spoke. Silas heard the words as clearly as if he stood beside the old fisherman. "Yes, Lord."

When Peter turned, Silas went out to him, trembling. "What are we to do?"

"I must go back to Rome."

Silas saw all the plans that had been made to protect Peter crumble. "If you do, you'll die there." *Lord, surely not this man.*

"Yes. I will die in Rome. As will Paul."

Tears welled in Silas's eyes. *Both of them, Lord?* "We need your voice, Peter."

"My voice?" He shook his head.

Silas knew better than to attempt to dissuade Peter from doing whatever the Lord willed. "As God wills, Peter. We will return to Rome together."

"No. *I* will return. You will remain behind."

Silas felt the blood leave his face. "I will not run for my life when my closest friends face death!" His voice broke.

Peter put a hand on his arm. "Is your life your own, Silas? We belong to the Lord. God has called *me* back to Rome. He will tell *you* what to do when the time comes."

"I can't let you go back alone!"

"I am not alone. The Lord is with me. Whatever happens, my friend, we are one in Christ Jesus. God causes everything to work together for the good of those who love God and are called according to His purpose."

"And if they crucify you?"

Peter shook his head. "I am not worthy to die in the same way the Lord did."

"They will do everything they can to break you, Peter. You know they will!"

"I know, Silas. Jesus told me years ago how I would die. You must pray for me, my friend. Pray I stand firm to the end." When Silas opened his mouth to argue further, Peter raised his hand. "No more, Silas. It is not for us to question the Lord's plan, my friend, but to follow it. I *must* go where God leads."

"I will not abandon you, Peter." Silas fought to keep his voice firm. "Before God, I swear it."

"I swore the same thing once." Peter's eyes shone with tears. "I didn't keep my vow."

Peter ordered the driver to turn the coach around. His wife insisted upon going back with him. "Wherever you go, I will go." Peter helped her into the coach and stepped up to sit beside her.

Determined not to be left behind, Silas climbed up. Peter shoved the pack of scrolls into his arms. The unbalanced weight made Silas step down. Scroll cases tumbled. As Silas scrambled for them, Peter closed and locked the coach door. He hit the side of the coach. The driver tapped the horses' flanks.

"Wait!"

Peter looked out at him. "May the Lord bless you and

protect you. May the Lord show you his favor and give you his peace."

Silas frantically retrieved scrolls, shoving them into the pack. *"Wait!"*

Slinging the pack over his shoulder, Silas ran to catch up. As he reached for the back of the coach, the driver gave a harsh cry and cracked his whip. The horses broke into a full gallop, leaving Silas choking in the dust.

ONE

SILAS sat at his writing table. His mind screamed *why?* as his dreams collapsed in grief and defeat. Clenching his hands, he tried to still the shaking. He dared not mix the ink or attempt to write now, for he would only ruin a section of new papyrus. He breathed in slowly, but could not calm his raging emotions.

"Lord, why does it always come to this?" Resting his elbows on the table, he covered his face with his hands. He could not blot out the horrific images.

Peter's wife screaming.

Peter calling out to her in anguish from where he was bound. *"Remember the Lord! Remember the Lord!"*

The Roman throng mocking the big fisherman from Galilee.

Silas groaned. *Oh, Lord. Even had I been blind, I would have heard the wrath of Satan against mankind in that arena, the lustful rejoicing at bloodshed. He murders men, and they help him do it!*

Silas felt pierced anew by the memory of seeing Christ crucified. At the time, Silas had questioned whether Jesus was the Messiah, but nonetheless he had been appalled by the cruelty of the Jews celebrating the death of a fellow Jew, that they could hate one of their own so much they would stand and mock him as he hung on the cross, beaten past recognition. They had stood sneering, calling out in contempt, "He saved others, but He can't save himself!"

Now, Silas tried to see past this world into the next, as Stephen had when members of the high council had stoned him outside the gates of Jerusalem. But all Silas saw was the darkness of men, the triumph of evil. *I am tired, Lord. I am sick of this life. All Your apostles, save John, are martyred. Is anyone else left who saw Your face?*

Lord, please take me home, I beg of You. Don't leave me here among these wretched people. I want to come home to You.

His eyes grew hot as he put shaking hands over his ears. "Forgive me, Lord. Forgive me. I'm afraid. I admit it. I'm terrified. Not of death, but of *dying.*" Even now, Silas could hear the echoes on Vatican Hill, where Nero's circus stood.

When his wife lay dead, Peter had bowed his head and wept.

The crowd had cheered when a cross was brought forth. "Yes! Crucify him! *Crucify him!*"

Peter's voice boomed above the noise. *"I am not worthy to die as my Lord did! I am not worthy!"*

"Coward!" Romans screamed. "He pleads for his life!"

Romans—so quick to worship courage—failed to recognize it in the man before them. They shrieked curses and cried out for further torture.

"Impale him!"

"Burn him alive!"

"Feed him to the lions!"

The big fisherman had left the shores of Galilee to throw the net of God's love to save masses drowning in sin. But the people swam in Satan's current. Peter had not asked for an *easier* death, only one *different* from the one his precious Lord had suffered.

Peter had never forgotten, had often recounted his failure to Silas. "The Lord said I would deny Him three times before the rooster crowed, and that's exactly what I did."

When the Romans nailed Peter to the cross, Silas had bowed his head. He couldn't watch.

Did I betray him the way he betrayed You, Lord? Did I fail him in his hour of need? When he looked again, he saw the centurion leaning down over Peter, listening. The Roman straightened, then stood for a moment before summoning two others. They levered up the cross and added ropes. Peter's body writhed in agony, but he made no sound.

The crew of soldiers strained at the task of turning the cross upside down.

The mob went quiet, and in that single moment Peter called out, his deep voice carrying up through the rows of spectators. "Forgive them, Father; they don't know what they are doing."

The Master's words.

Tears had welled in Silas's eyes.

It had taken all his will to stand in the arch in the upper corridor and keep his eyes fixed upon Peter in his suffering. "Pray when I face my death, Silas," Peter had requested weeks before his capture. "Pray that I will remain faithful to the end."

And so Silas had prayed, fiercely, determined, in anguish, in fear. *Lord, if it ever comes to this for me, let me in faith endure to the end as Peter did. Do not let me recant what I know! You are the way, the truth, and the life. Lord, give my friend comfort in his agony. Lord, give Your beloved servant Peter strength to cling tightly to his faith in You. Lord, let him see You as Stephen did! Fill him with the joy of homecoming. Speak to him now, Lord. Please say those words we all long to hear: "Well done, my good and faithful servant."*

He was, Lord. Your servant Peter was faithful.

God, I beg of You, let this be the last execution I witness!

Last night Silas had awakened, certain he heard Paul's voice dictating another letter. Relieved, joyous, he had jumped up. "Paul!" The dream was so vivid it took a moment for the truth to strike him. When it did, it felt like a physical blow. *Paul's dead.*

Silas put his hands flat on the writing table. "You are the resurrection and the life." He must remind himself. "The resurrection." What were the words John had said when they last met in Ephesus? "Anyone who believes in Jesus will have . . ." *No. That isn't right.* "Anyone who believes in God's Son *has* eternal life." Paul's words echoed in his mind. "While we were utterly helpless, Christ died for us sinners." John's conviction cried out to him. "Love each other . . ."

A shout from outside made Silas stiffen. Were they coming for him now? Would he face another imprisonment, another flogging, more torture? *If I try to escape suffering by telling them I'm a Roman citizen, will that make me a coward? It's true, but I despise everything about this empire. I hate that even in the smallest way I'm part of it. Lord, I was strong once. I was. Not anymore . . .*

Paul's voice echoed again. "When I am weak, then I am strong. . . ."

Silas gripped his head. "You, my friend, not I . . ."

He could not think clearly here in the confines of Rome with the cacophony of voices, trampling feet, vendors' cries. The mob, the ever insatiable mob on his heels. *I have to get out of here! I have to get away from this place!*

He scrambled to gather his writing materials and few possessions. The scrolls! He must safeguard the scrolls!

Heart pounding, Silas left the small, stifling room.

The proprietor spotted him the moment he came out the door, as though the man had been watching for him. "You there!" He crossed the narrow street. "You're leaving?"

"My business here is finished."

"You don't look well. Perhaps you should stay a few more days."

Silas glanced at him. The man cared nothing about his health. Money was all the man wanted—more money.

The noise of humanity seemed to grow louder around Silas. Wolf faces everywhere. Romulus and Remus's offspring filled the street. Silas looked at the people milling about, talking, shouting, laughing, arguing. The poor lived here—huddled, hungry masses that needed so much more than food. They reeked of discontent, cursing one another over the least provocation. These were the people Rome appeased with blood sport. It kept their minds from dwelling on the lack of grain.

Silas looked into the proprietor's eyes. Paul would have spoken the words of life to him. Peter would have spoken of Jesus.

"What?" The proprietor frowned.

Let him die, Silas thought. *Why should I cast pearls before this pig?* "Perhaps I've got the fever," he said. "It swept through the village where I stayed a few weeks ago." True enough. Better than saying, "I went to the games three days ago, and watched two of my closest friends executed. All I want now is to get as far away from this wretched city as I can. And if the whole population of Rome is sucked down to hell, I will stand and shout praises to God for their destruction!"

As Silas expected, the proprietor drew back in alarm. "Fever? Yes, you must go."

"Yes, I must." Silas smiled tightly. "Plagues spread quickly in narrow streets, don't they?" *Especially the plague of sin.* "I paid for a week, didn't I?"

The man blanched. "I don't remember."

"I didn't think you would." Silas shouldered his pack and walked away.

✦   ✦   ✦

After several days of walking, Silas reached Puteoli. He did not have the stamina he once had, nor the heart.

He made his way to the harbor and wandered in the marketplace. *Where do I go from here, Lord?* Semaphores flashed, signaling the arrival of grain ships, probably from Egypt. Workers hurried past him, hastening to unload sacks of grain, carry them to the *mensores* for weighing. Other vessels anchored farther out, *lenuncularii* operating tenders between ship and shore. Merchandise came from all over the empire to satisfy the Roman markets: corn, cattle, wine, and wool from Sicily; horses from Spain; slaves from Britannia and Germania; marble from Greece; multicolored rugs from Asshur. The port was a good place to lose himself and still find what he most needed.

The scents made Silas's head swim: salt-sea air, animal dung, spices, wine, and human sweat. Seagulls screeched overhead as fish were piled on a cart. Criers shouted goods for sale. Sheep bleated from holding pens. Wild dogs from Britannia snarled from crates. Foreign slaves stood naked on platforms, sweating in the sun as they were auctioned. One fought against his bonds while a woman and child were pulled away. Though he shouted in a strange language, his anguish was well understood. The woman's weeping turned to hysterical screams as her child was wrenched from her. She tried to reach him, but was dragged in another direction. The child wailed in terror, arms outstretched toward his mother.

Throat tight, Silas turned away. He couldn't escape

injustice and misery. It was all around him, threatening
to suffocate him. The seed of sin planted centuries ago in
the Garden of Eden had taken root and spread its shoots of
wickedness everywhere. And all feasted on this poisonous
fruit that would bring them nothing but death.

It was late afternoon when he saw a familiar symbol
carved into a post of a booth filled with barrels of olives
and baskets of pomegranates, dates, figs, and nuts. His
stomach growled. His mouth watered. He hadn't eaten anything since leaving The Three Taverns two days ago.

He listened to the proprietor bargain with a woman.
"You know these are the best dates in all the empire."

"And you know I cannot pay such a high price."

Neither shouted nor grew vitriolic, a common occur-
rence in marketplaces. She made an offer; he countered.
She shook her head and made another offer. He laughed
and made yet another. When they reached agreement,
the proprietor grabbed a handful of dried dates and put
them on his scale. He wrapped them in a cloth the woman
handed him and received payment. As she walked away,
he turned his attention to Silas. "Olives? Dates?"

Silas shook his head. He had spent his last coin on
bread. He looked at the symbol carved into the pole. Had
this grinning pirate put it there? Before he could find
a way to ask, the man cocked his head and frowned. "I
know you. Don't I?"

"We've never met."

"You look familiar."

Silas's heart pounded. He thought of turning away, but
where would he go? "I am a friend of Theophilus."

The man's eyes cleared. "Ah!" He grinned. "How is he
these days?"

"Not well." Silas took a step back, thinking he might have made a mistake in saying anything to this man.

The merchant glanced one way and then the other and beckoned Silas closer. "Silas. Is that not your name?"

Silas blanched.

"Do not look distressed, my friend," the man said quickly. He dropped his voice. "I heard you preach once, in Corinth. Years ago—five, maybe six. You look tired. Are you hungry?"

Silas couldn't answer.

The man grabbed some dates and figs and pressed them into Silas's hand. "Go to the end of the street; turn left. Follow that street to the end. It will wind like a serpent before you reach your destination. Pass two fountains. Take the first street on the right just after. Knock on the door of the third house. Ask for Epanetus."

Could he remember all that, or would he find himself wandering Puteoli all night? "Whom shall I say sent me?"

"My apologies. In my excitement at meeting you, I forgot to introduce myself." He laughed. "I'm Urbanus." He leaned forward and said gruffly, "You are an answer to many prayers."

Silas felt the weight of the man's expectations. "Peter is dead."

Urbanus gave a solemn nod. "We heard."

So soon? "How?"

"Bad news travels fast. Our brother Patrobas arrived day before yesterday. He could not find you in the catacombs."

Patrobas. Silas knew him well. "I feared someone might follow and others be taken."

"We feared you had been arrested." Urbanus grasped Silas's arms. "God has answered our prayers. You are well.

We did not expect the added blessing of your presence here."

Blessing? This man remembered his face from one encounter. What if others, enemies, also recognized him as Peter's scribe? His presence might endanger these brothers and sisters.

Lord, will all we've worked for be destroyed in a bloodbath?

Urbanus leaned closer. "Do not look so troubled, my friend. Puteoli is a busy city. Everyone has an eye to business and little else. People come; people go." He repeated the directions, slowly this time. "I would show you the way myself, but I cannot entrust my booth to others. They're all thieves . . . just as I once was." He laughed again and slapped Silas on the shoulder. "Go. I will see you later." He called to a group of women passing by. "Come! See what good olives I have! The best in the empire!"

Urbanus did not lie. Two dates and a fig took the sharp edge of hunger away, and they did taste better than anything Silas had eaten in Rome. He kept the rest in the pouch tied to his belt.

The day was hot, and Silas felt sweat trickle down his back as he walked. Merchants' booths gave way to streets lined with tenements. Shoulders aching, he shifted his pack. Over the years, he had carried far heavier loads than this, but the weight of the scrolls seemed to increase with every step.

A servant opened the door when he knocked. The Ethiopian's inscrutable gaze took Silas in from dusty head to sandaled feet.

"I am looking for the house of Epanetus."

"This is the house of Epanetus. Who may I tell my master is come?"

"A friend of Theophilus."

The servant opened the door wider. "I am Macombo. Come. Enter in." He closed the door firmly behind Silas. "Wait here." He strode away.

It was the house of a rich man. Pillared corridors and frescoed walls. An open court with a white marble statue of a woman pouring water from an urn. The sound of the water made Silas realize his thirst. He swallowed hard and longed to shrug the pack from his shoulders and sit.

Footsteps approached—the hurried slap of sandals. A tall, broad-shouldered man strode across the courtyard. His short-cropped hair was gray, his features strongly carved. "I am Epanetus."

"Urbanus sent me."

"Which Urbanus would that be?"

Caution was to be expected. "From the agora." Silas opened his pouch and took out a handful of plump dates.

Epanetus laughed. "Ah, yes. 'The best dates and figs in all the empire.'" He extended his hands. "You are welcome here."

Silas received the greeting, knowing his own response was somewhat less enthusiastic.

"Come." Epanetus gave a quiet order to Macombo and then led Silas across the court, through an archway, and into another area of the house. Several people sat in a large room. Silas recognized one of them.

Patrobas came swiftly to his feet. "Silas!" Grinning broadly, he came to embrace him. "We feared you were lost to us." He drew back and kept one hand firmly on Silas's arm as he addressed the others. "God has answered our prayers."

They surrounded him. The heartfelt greetings broke

down Silas's last defenses. Shoulders sagging, he bowed his head and wept.

No one spoke for a moment, and then they all spoke at once.

"Pour him a little wine."

"You're exhausted."

"Sit. Have something to eat."

"Macombo, set the tray here."

Patrobas frowned and guided Silas. "Rest here."

When someone took hold of his pack, Silas instinctively gripped it tighter. "No!"

"You are safe here," Epanetus said. "Consider my home yours."

Silas felt ashamed. "I must safeguard these scrolls."

"Put the pack here beside you," Patrobas said. "No one will touch it unless you give permission."

Exhausted, Silas sat. He saw nothing but love and compassion in the faces surrounding him. A woman looked up at him, eyes welling with tears. Her concern pierced him. "Letters." He managed to shrug the pack from his shoulders and set it down beside him. "Copies of those Paul sent to the Corinthians. And Peter's." His voice broke. Covering his face, he tried to regain control and couldn't. His shoulders shook with his sobs.

Someone squeezed his shoulder. They wept with him, their love leaving no room for embarrassment.

"Our friend is with the Lord." Patrobas's voice was thick with grief.

"Yes. No one can harm him or his wife now."

"They stand in the Lord's presence as we speak."

As I long to be, Silas wanted to cry out. *Oh, to see Jesus' face again!* To have an end of trials, an end to fear, an end to the attack of doubt when he least expected it. *I am losing the battle inside myself, Lord.*

"We must hold firm to that which we know is true."

Paul's words, spoken so long ago. They had been sitting in a dungeon, darkness surrounding them, their bodies laced with pain from a brutal whipping. "Hold fast," he had said.

"I'm trying," Silas moaned.

"What is he saying?"

Silas mumbled into his hands. "Jesus died for our sins and was raised from the grave on the third day. . . ." But all he could see was the Lord on the cross, Paul beheaded, Peter crucified. He pressed the heels of his hands into his eyes.

"He's ill."

"Shhhh . . ."

"Silas." A firm hand this time, a Roman hand. A tray laden with food was set before him. Epanetus and Patrobas encouraged him to eat. Silas took bread in trembling hands and tore it. *This is My body. . . .* He held the two halves, shaking. "Do I dare eat of it?"

Whispers of concern.

Epanetus poured wine into a cup and held it out to him. "Drink." Silas stared at the red fluid. *This is My blood. . . .* He remembered Jesus on the cross, blood and water pouring from the spear wound in His side. He remembered Peter hanging upside down.

Pain gripped his chest. His heart raced faster and faster. The room grew dark.

"Silas!"

He heard the roaring of the Roman mob. Hands grabbed hold of him. *So be it, Lord. If I die, there will be an end of suffering. And rest. Please, Lord. Let me rest.*

"Silas . . ." A woman's voice this time. Close. He felt her breath on his face. "Don't leave us. . . ."

Voices above and around him, and then no sound at all.

+ + +

Silas roused, confused. A clay lamp burned on a stand. Someone came close. A cool hand rested on his brow. Silas groaned and closed his eyes. His throat squeezed tight and hot.

A strong arm slid beneath him and raised him. "Drink." Macombo held a cup to Silas's lips.

Something warm and sweetened with honey.

"A little more. It will help you sleep."

Silas remembered and struggled to rise. "Where are they? Where . . . ? The letters!"

"Here." Macombo lifted the pack.

Silas took it and clutched it close, sighing as he lay back on the bed.

"No one will take anything from you, Silas."

Voices came and went, along with dreams. Paul spoke to him across a campfire. Luke dressed his wounds. They sang as they followed the Roman road. He awakened to footsteps and fell asleep again. Paul paced, agitated, and Silas shook his head. "If you will but rest, my friend, and pray, the words will come."

Voices again, familiar now. Macombo and Epanetus.

"To whom does he speak?"

"I don't know."

"Silas . . ."

He opened his eyes. A woman stood with the sunlight at her back. When she came close, he frowned. "I don't know you."

"I'm Diana. You've been sleeping a long time."

"Diana . . ." He tried to remember. He had seen her face, but where?

She put her hand on his shoulder. "I'll just sit with you awhile."

"How is he?" Epanetus spoke from somewhere close.

"He has no fever."

"Pain?"

"His dreams trouble him."

Time passed; how much, Silas didn't know or care. He awakened again to voices in the corridor outside the room.

"It's not just exhaustion that makes him sleep so long. It's grief."

"Give him time. He will find his strength in the Lord."

Murmuring and then Macombo's voice. "He seems little interested in food or drink."

"I heard him speak in Corinth," said Urbanus, the pirate merchant who sold the best dates in the empire. "He was magnificent. Think of the honor the Lord has bestowed on us by sending him here. Silas saw Jesus in the flesh."

"And saw Him crucified." Patrobas spoke with quiet firmness.

"And risen! We've only heard about the Lord. We never saw Him face-to-face. We never ate with Him or walked with Him. . . ."

Silas put his arm over his eyes.

"Let him rest a little longer before you try to wake him. It's only been three days, and he's endured more than any of us. . . ."

Three days! No matter how much Silas might long to escape the sorrow of this world, he could not will himself to heaven. He reached down. The pack of precious scrolls lay beside him. His body ached as he sat up. He rubbed his face. His joints and muscles screamed as he stood. He rolled his shoulders and stretched slowly. Raising his hands in habitual praise, he prayed. "This is a day that You have made, Lord, and I will rejoice in it." He might not feel like it, but he would do so in obedience. Grudging obedience.

Dogged, determined, he picked up the pack and followed the sound of retreating voices. He stood in the archway of a large room. Men and women of all ages sat together, enjoying a meal. Silas stayed in the shadowed corridor, studying them. He saw meat on a fine pottery platter, and fruit being passed in a simple, woven basket. Everyone had brought something to share.

A love feast.

Silas remembered the gatherings in Jerusalem, the first year after Jesus ascended, the excitement, the joy, the openhanded charity between brothers and sisters.

Jerusalem! How he longed to go home to those halcyon days.

But even if he could go back to Judea, he knew nothing would be the same. Persecution had driven the followers of Jesus to other cities and provinces, leaving behind Jewish factions that constantly warred with one another. One day, Rome would make peace for them, with the army, the way Rome always made peace. If only they would listen!

Jesus had warned of Jerusalem's destruction. John had told Luke what Jesus said, and Luke had written it all down in the history he was collecting. The good doctor had been hard at work on it during the years Silas had known him, when they both traveled with Paul. A kind man, educated, inquisitive. A gifted physician. Paul would have died several times if not for Luke's ministrations. *And I along with him.*

Had Luke escaped from Rome? Had he gone back to Corinth or Ephesus?

Timothy's most recent letter said John was living in Ephesus. Mary, Jesus' mother, lived with him. Her sons, James and Jude, who became believers when they saw the risen Christ, had joined the apostles on the council in Jerusalem.

"Silas!"

Startled from his reverie, Silas saw Epanetus cross the room. "Come. Join us." Patrobas rose, as did several others.

Epanetus led Silas to a place of honor. Diana rose and prepared a plate of food for him. She smiled into his eyes when he thanked her. A young man sitting beside her whispered in her ear. "Not now, Curiatus," she replied.

Everyone talked at once, until Epanetus laughed and raised his hands. "Quiet, everyone! Give Silas time to eat before we attack him with questions."

They talked among themselves again, but Silas felt their glances. He gave silent thanks to God for what was placed before him. Pork, and judging by the quality, from a pig fattened in oak forests. A Roman delicacy, and unclean by Mosaic law. He took some fruit instead. Even now, after years of being freed from the Mosaic law, he had difficulty eating pork.

Others arrived—a family with several children, a young couple, two older men . . . The room filled. And each wanted to meet him, to clasp his hand.

Silas felt alone in the midst of them, trapped inside himself, captive to thoughts that buzzed like angry bees. He longed for solitude, and knew how ungrateful it would be to rise and leave them now. And where could he go other than that silent room with its rich surroundings that reminded him of things he had worked so hard to forget?

Everyone had finished eating, and he lost his appetite. He saw their expectation, felt their hunger to hear him speak.

The boy spoke first. "You knew the Lord Jesus, didn't you?" He ignored his mother's hand on his arm. "Would you tell us about Him?"

And then the others began. "Tell us everything, Silas."

"What was He like?"

"How did He look?"

"What did you feel when you were in His presence?"

"And the apostles? You knew them all, didn't you? What were they like?" The boy again, all eyes and pleading. "Will you teach us as you've taught others?"

Hadn't he preached hundreds of times in dozens of towns from Jerusalem to Antioch to Thessalonica? Hadn't he told the story of Jesus crucified and risen to small crowds and large, some praising God, others mocking and hostile? Hadn't he worked with Timothy in teaching the Corinthians? He had traveled thousands of miles alongside Paul, establishing churches in city after city.

Yet, here among these friendly, hospitable brothers and sisters, he could think of nothing to say.

Silas looked from one face to another, trying to sort his thoughts, trying to think where to start, when all he could see in his mind's eye was Peter hanging upside down, his blood forming a growing pool beneath him.

Everyone was looking at him, waiting, eager.

"I fear . . ." His voice broke. He felt as though someone had clamped strong hands around his throat. He swallowed convulsively and waited until the sensation passed. "I fear I endanger you." He spoke the truth, but doubted it commended him. "Paul is beheaded; Peter crucified. The apostles are scattered, most martyred. No one can replace these great witnesses of God. No one can speak the message of Christ as effectively as they have."

"You spoke effectively in Corinth," Urbanus said. "Your every word pierced my heart."

"The Holy Spirit pierces you, not I. And that was a long time ago, when I was younger and stronger than I am today." Stronger in body; stronger in faith. His eyes blurred with tears. "A few days ago in Rome, I watched a dear friend die a horrible death because he carried the testimony of God. I don't think I can go on. . . ."

"You were Peter's secretary," Patrobas said.

Leading words. They wanted to draw him out into the open.

"Yes, and my presence brings danger to all of you."

"A danger we welcome, Silas." The others murmured agreement with Epanetus's firm declaration.

"Please. Teach us." The boy spoke again.

He was not much younger than Timothy had been the first time Silas met him. Diana looked at him with her beautiful dark eyes, so full of compassion. His heart squeezed at the sight. What could he say to make them understand what he didn't understand himself? *Oh, Lord, I can't talk about crucifixion. I can't talk about the cross . . . not Yours or Peter's.*

He shook his head, eyes downcast. "I regret, I cannot think clearly enough to teach." He fumbled with the pack beside him. "But I've brought letters." Exact copies he had made from originals. He looked at Epanetus, desperate, appealing to him as host. "Perhaps someone here can read the letters."

"Yes. Of course." Smiling, Epanetus rose.

Silas took one out and, with shaking hand, presented it to the Roman.

Epanetus read one of Paul's letters to the Corinthians. When he finished, he held the scroll for a moment before carefully rolling it and giving it back to Silas. "We have yearned for such meat as this."

Silas carefully tucked the scroll away.

"Can we read another?" Curiatus had moved closer.

"Pick one."

Patrobas read one of Peter's letters. Silas had made many copies of it and sent them to many of the churches he had helped Paul start.

"Peter makes it clear you were a great help to him, Silas."

Silas was touched by Diana's praise, and wary because of his feelings. "The words are Peter's."

"Beautifully written in Greek," Patrobas pointed out. "Hardly Peter's native language."

What could he say without sounding boastful? Yes, he had helped Peter refine his thoughts and put them into proper Greek. Peter had been a fisherman, working to put food on his family's table. While Peter had toiled over his nets, Silas had sat in comfort, yoked to an exacting rabbi who demanded every word of the Torah be memorized. God had chosen Peter as one of His twelve companions. And Peter had chosen Silas to be his secretary. By God's grace and mercy, Silas had accompanied Peter and his wife on their journey to Rome. He would be forever humbled and thankful for the years he spent with them.

Though Aramaic was the common language of Judea, Silas could speak and write Hebrew and Greek as well as Latin. He spoke Egyptian enough to get by in conversation.

Every day, he thanked God that he had been allowed to use what gifts he had to serve the Lord's servants.

"What was it like to walk with Jesus?"

The boy again. Insatiable youth. So much like Timothy. "I did not travel with Him, nor was I among those He chose."

"But you knew Him."

"I knew *of* Him. Twice, I met Him and spoke with Him. I know Him now as Savior and Lord, just as you do. He abides in me, and I in Him through the Holy Spirit." He put his hand against his chest. *Lord, Lord, would I have the faith of Peter to endure if I were nailed to a cross?*

"Are you all right, Silas? Are you in pain again?"

He shook his head. He was in no physical danger. Not here. Not now.

"How many of the twelve disciples did you know?"

"What were they like?"

So many questions—the same ones he'd answered countless times before in casual gatherings from Antioch to Rome.

"He knew them all," Patrobas said into the silence. "He sat on the Jerusalem council."

Silas forced his mind to focus. "They were strangers to me during the years Jesus preached." Jesus' closest companions were not people with whom Silas would have wanted contact. Fishermen, a zealot, a tax collector. He would have avoided their company, for any commerce with them would have damaged his reputation. It was only later that they became his beloved brothers. "I heard Jesus speak once near the shores of Galilee and several times at the Temple."

Curiatus leaned forward, resting his elbows on his knees

and his chin in his hands. "What was it like to be in His presence?"

"The first time I met Him, I thought He was a young rabbi wise beyond His years. But when He spoke and I looked into His eyes, I was afraid." He shook his head, thinking back. "Not afraid. Terrified."

"But He was kind and merciful. So we've been told."

"So He is."

"What did He look like?"

"I heard He glowed like gold and fire poured from His lips."

"On a mountain once, Peter, James, and John saw Him transfigured, but Jesus left His glory behind and came to us as a man. I saw Him several times. There was nothing in Jesus' physical appearance to attract people to Him. But when He spoke, He did so with the full authority of God." Silas's thoughts drifted to those days before He knew the Lord personally, days filled with rumors, whispered questions, while the priests gathered in tight circles, grumbling in Temple corridors. It had been their behavior most of all that sent Silas to Galilee to see for himself who this Jesus was. He had sensed their fear and later witnessed their ferocious jealousy.

Epanetus put his hand on Silas's shoulder. "Enough, my friends. Silas is tired. And it is late."

As the others rose, the boy pressed between two men and came to him. "Can I talk with you? Just for a little while."

Diana reached for him, cheeks flushed, eyes full of apology. "You heard Epanetus, my son. Come. The meeting is over for the evening. Give the man rest." She drew her son away.

"Could we come back tomorrow?"

"Later. Perhaps. After work . . ."

Curiatus glanced back. "You won't leave, will you? You have words of truth to speak."

"Curiatus!"

"He wrote all those scrolls, Mother. He could write all he's seen and heard. . . ."

Diana put her arm around her son and spoke softly, but with more firmness this time, as she led him from the room.

Epanetus saw everyone safely away. When he returned, he smiled. "Curiatus is right. It would be a good thing if you would write a record."

Silas had spent most of his life writing letters, putting down onto scrolls the encouragement and instructions of men inspired by God. The council in Jerusalem, James, Paul, Peter. "For the most part, I helped others sort and express their thoughts."

"Would it not help you to sort your thoughts and feelings if you did? You suffer, Silas. We all can see that. You loved Peter and his wife. You loved Paul. It is never easy to lose a friend. And you've lost many."

"My faith is weak."

"Perhaps that is the best of all reasons for you to dwell on the past." Epanetus spoke more seriously. "You have lived your life in service to others. Your ink-stained fingers are proof of it."

The darkest part of night had come, a darkness that crushed Silas's spirit. He looked down at his hands. They indicted him.

"Curiatus is named aptly." Epanetus spoke gently. "But perhaps God brought you to us and put the idea in the boy's head. Is that not possible?"

Silas closed his eyes. *Can I dwell on the past without being undone by it? I regret, Lord; I regret the wasted years. Is that a sin, too?*

Epanetus spread his hands. "Precious few are left who were in Judea when Jesus walked this earth."

"That's all too painfully true." Silas heard his bitterness.

Epanetus sat, hands clasped, expression intense. "I will not share my story until I know you better, but know this: you are not alone in your struggle with faith. Whatever sorrow you carry other than the death of your friends is not hidden from the Lord. You know and I know Jesus died for all our sins and rose from the dead. Through faith in Him we have the promise of everlasting life. We will live forever in the presence of the Lord. But like the boy, I crave to know more about Jesus. So much of what we hear drifts away. Those scrolls, for example. Patrobas and I read two tonight. But if you leave tomorrow, how much will we all remember by next week or next month? And what of our children?"

"Another has already set about the task of writing the history: Luke, the physician."

"I have heard of him. That's wonderful news, Silas, but where is he now? He left Rome after Paul was beheaded, didn't he? How long before we receive a copy of what he has written?"

"He was not the only one. Many have undertaken the task of compiling an account of things that happened and what's been accomplished."

"That may be so, Silas, but we have received nothing in the way of letters, other than the one written by Paul. You are here with us! We want to know what you learned from Peter and Paul. We want to see these men of faith as you did. They endured to the end. As you endure now. Share your life with us."

"What you ask is a monumental task!" *And I'm so weary, Lord. Let someone else do what he asks.*

"The task is not beyond your abilities, Silas." Epanetus gripped his arm. "Whatever you need, you have only to ask. Scrolls, ink, a safe place to write without interruption. God has blessed me with abundance so that I might bless others. Give me the blessing and honor to serve you." The Roman stood. "May you be at peace with whatever God asks of you."

"Epanetus!" Silas called out before he left him alone in the room. "It is not easy to look back."

"I know." The Roman stood in the doorway, mouth tipped. "But sometimes we must look back before we can move forward."

SILAS, *a disciple of Jesus Christ, eyewitness to the Crucifixion, servant of the risen Lord and Savior, Jesus Christ, to the family of Theophilus. Grace to you and peace from God our Father and the Lord Jesus Christ.*

The first time I heard the name of Jesus was in the Temple in Jerusalem. Rumors of false prophets and self-proclaimed messiahs were common in those days, and priests were often called upon to investigate. A few years earlier, Theudas had claimed to be the anointed one of God. He gained four hundred disciples before he was slain by the Romans. The rest dispersed. Then, during the census, Judas of Galilee rose up. Soon, he too was dead and his followers scattered. My father had warned me against men who grew like weeds among wheat. "Trust in the law of Moses, my son. It is a lamp to guide your feet and a light for your path."

John the Baptist began gathering crowds at the Jordan River, baptizing for the repentance of sins. A delegation of priests went out to question him. Upon their return, I overheard angry words in the hallowed corridors.

"He's a false prophet who comes out of the wilderness and lives off locusts and honey."

"The man is mad!"

"The man wears a garment of camel's hair and a leather belt!"

"He dared call us a brood of snakes."

"Mad or not, he has the people listening to him. And he cried out against us, asking who'd warned us against God's coming wrath. We must do something about him!"

Something was done, but not by the priests and religious

leaders. John confronted King Herod for his adulterous relationship with Herodias, his brother Philip's wife. Arrested,
he was held in the palace dungeon. Herodias held a celebration for the king's birthday and used her daughter to entice
Herod into making a foolish promise: if she would dance
for his guests, he would give her whatever she wanted. The
trap closed. The girl demanded John the Baptist's head on a
platter, and happily gave the gruesome gift to her scheming
mother.

Those who thought John the Baptist was the Messiah
grieved over his death and lost hope. Others said he pointed
the way to Jesus, and went after the rabbi from Nazareth.
Some, like me, waited cautiously to see what happened. All
Jews lived in hope of the Messiah's coming. We longed to
see the chains of Rome broken, and our oppressors driven
from the land God had given our ancestors. We wanted our
nation to be great again, as it had been during the time of
King David and King Solomon, his son.

Some buried their hope in the shallow grave of a false messiah only to have it arise again when a new one appeared on
the horizon. Hope can be a terrible taskmaster!

There were many rabbis in Judea, each with disciples
yoked to his teachings. Some met in the corridors of the
Temple, others in distant synagogues. Some traveled from
town to town, gathering disciples as they went. It was not
uncommon to see a group of young men following in their
rabbi's footsteps, hanging on his every word.

I thought none so wise as my father, who had told me to
memorize the Law and live by it. I thought the Law would
save me. I thought by following the commandments, and giving sacrifices, I could garner God's favor. Hence, I was often
in the Temple, bringing my tithes and offerings. The Law

was my delight, and my bane. I prayed and fasted. I obeyed the commandments. And still I felt I existed on the edge of a great precipice. One slip, and I would fall into sin and be lost forever. I longed for assurance.

Or thought I did.

The stories about Jesus persisted and grew in magnitude.

"Jesus gave sight to a blind man!"

"Jesus made a paralyzed man walk in Capernaum."

"He cast out demons!"

Some even claimed He raised a widow's son from the dead.

The leading priests who had gone out to investigate John the Baptist met in chambers with the high priest, Caiaphas. My father, who had been a longtime friend of Annas's family, told me later how incensed they became when it was asked if Jesus might be the Messiah.

"The Messiah will be a son of David born in Bethlehem, not some lowly carpenter from Nazareth who eats with tax collectors and prostitutes!"

Neither they, nor I, knew at the time that Jesus had in fact been born in Bethlehem of a virgin betrothed to Joseph. Both Mary and Joseph were of the tribe of Judah and descendants of the great King David. Further evidence came when Isaiah's prophesy was fulfilled, for Mary had conceived by the Holy Spirit. These facts became known to me later and merely affirmed all I had, by then, come to believe about Jesus. To my knowledge, nothing ever changed the minds of Annas, Caiaphas, and other priests who clutched so tightly to the power they imagined they held in the palms of their hands. Annas is dead now. And Caiaphas too is long gone.

What kept me away from Jesus for so long was the company

He kept. I had never heard of any rabbi eating with sinners, let alone inviting them to be His friends. I pursued discipleship with a well-respected rabbi and was not received by him until I proved myself worthy to be his student. Jesus went out and chose His disciples from among common men. I had spent my life in caution, avoiding all those things the Torah declared unclean. I did not converse with women, and I never allowed a Gentile into my house. I knew my rabbi would not hear the name of Jesus. The Nazarene was a renegade. Jesus healed lepers. Jesus taught the women who traveled with Him. He gathered the poor, the downtrodden, the defiled on hillsides and fed them. He even preached to hated Samaritans!

Who was this man? And what good did He think He was doing by shattering the traditions accumulated over the centuries?

I longed to discuss all these matters with my father, but could not. He was too ill and died in the heat of summer. I sought out one of his most respected friends, a member of the high council, Nicodemus. "Is the Nazarene a prophet or a dangerous revolutionary?"

"He speaks with great compassion and knows the Law."

I was astounded. "You have met the man?"

"Once. Briefly." He changed the subject and would not be drawn back to it.

I wondered how many others among the leading priests and scribes had gone out to hear Jesus preach. Every time Jesus' name was mentioned, I listened. I learned He spoke in many synagogues and taught about the Kingdom of God. The desire to leave my careful life grew in me. I wanted to see Jesus. I wanted to hear Him preach. I wanted to know if He was the one who could answer all my questions.

Most of all, like many others, I wanted to see Him perform a miracle. Perhaps then I would know whether to take this particular prophet seriously or not.

So I went to Galilee.

+   +   +

The crowd in Capernaum felt bigger than any I had seen at the Temple, except during the Passover celebration, when Jews came from Mesopotamia, Cappadocia, Pontus, Asia, Phrygia, Pamphylia, Egypt, and even Rome. The people I found in Capernaum that day frightened me, for they were wretched. A blind man in rags, destitute widows, mothers holding crying children, cripples, people dragging stretchers on which lay sick relatives or friends, lepers and outcasts, all calling out and trying to push forward and get closer to Jesus. Of course, I had seen many poor and sick begging on the Temple steps, and often gave them money. But never had I seen so many! They filled the streets and spilled down to the shoreline of the Sea of Galilee.

"Jesus!" Someone shouted. "Jesus is coming!"

Everyone began to call out to Him at once. The sound of anguished, pleading, hopeful voices was deafening.

"My father is sick. . . ."

"My brother is dying. . . ."

"I'm blind. Heal me!"

"Help me, Jesus!"

"My sister is demon-possessed!"

"Jesus!"

"Jesus!"

I stretched up, but could not see over the people. My heart raced with excitement as I caught their fever of hope. Hauling myself onto the wall, I stood precariously balanced, desperate to see this man so many called a prophet, and some said was the Messiah.

And there He was, moving through the people. My heart sank.

Jesus was not like any rabbi I had ever seen. This was no gray-haired scholar with flowing white robes and scowling face. He was young—no more than a few years older than I. He wore simple, homespun garments, and had the broad shoulders, strong arms, and dark skin of a common laborer. Nothing in His appearance commended Him. Jesus looked at those around Him. He even touched some. One grasped Jesus' hand, kissing it and weeping. Jesus moved on through the crowd as people cried out in joy. "A miracle!"

Where? I wondered. *Where is the miracle?*

People tried to reach over others. "Touch me, Jesus! Touch me!" His friends moved closer to Him, trying to keep the people back. The eldest—Peter—shouted for them to make room. Jesus stepped into one of the boats. Disappointment filled me. Had I come so far to have only a glimpse of Him?

Jesus sat in the bow as His disciples rowed. They had not gone far when they dropped anchor. Jesus spoke from there, and the crowd grew quiet. They sat and listened as His calm voice carried across the water.

I cannot tell you all that Jesus said that day, or His exact words, but His teaching caused great turmoil within me. He said the heart of the Law was mercy; I had always thought it was judgment. He spoke of loving our enemies, but I could not believe He meant the Romans who had brought idols into the land. He said not to worry about the future, for each day had trouble enough. I worried all the time about keeping the Law. I worried that I would not live up to my father's expectations. I worried from morning to night about a hundred inconsequential things. Jesus warned us against false prophets, while the scribes and Pharisees looked upon Him as one.

Jesus' voice was deep and flowed like many waters. My heart trembled at the sound of it. Even now after so many years, I wait to hear His voice again.

When He finished speaking, the people rose and cried out, not for more of His wisdom, but demanding miracles. They wanted healing! They wanted bread! They wanted an end to Roman domination!

"Be our king!"

Peter raised the sail. Andrew drew up the anchor. People waded into the water, but the wind had already moved the boat well away from shore.

I wanted to cry out, too; not for bread, of which I had plenty, nor for healing, of which I had no need, but for His interpretation of the Law. His words had filled me with more questions than those that had brought me to Galilee. From boyhood, I had listened to scribes and religious leaders. Never had a man spoken with authority like the carpenter from Nazareth.

When people ran along the shore, I gathered my robes, shed my dignity, and ran with them. The boat turned and sailed toward the distant shore. Others kept running, intending to reach the other side of the lake before He did.

Weary, out of breath, I sat, arms resting on my raised knees, and watched Jesus sail away, taking my hope with Him.

✦   ✦   ✦

Jesus traveled from town to town. He spoke in the synagogues. He spoke to growing crowds on hillsides. He taught through stories the common people understood better than I, stories about soil, seeds, wheat and weeds, hidden treasure in a field, fishing nets, things unfamiliar to someone who had grown up in Jerusalem. People argued over Him constantly. Some said He was from heaven; others refused to believe He was even a prophet. Scribes and Pharisees demanded a miraculous sign, and Jesus refused.

"Only an evil and adulterous generation would demand a miraculous sign; but the only sign I will give them is the sign of the prophet Jonah."

But what did that mean?

Many disciples left Jesus, some out of disappointment, others because they could not understand or believe.

I left out of fear of what the religious leaders might do if they saw me among Jesus' followers. I had my reputation to protect.

"Did you find the Messiah?" My rabbi mocked me.

"No," I said, and soon after left him.

Jesus came to Jerusalem and taught in the Temple, much to the ire of the scribes and Pharisees. They questioned Him, and he confounded them with His answers. They set traps; He sprang them. They asked trick questions about the Law, and He exposed their deceit, challenged their knowledge of the Torah, and said they did not serve God, but their father, the devil.

The city was alive with excitement. Everyone was talking about Jesus.

And then, He was gone again, out in the countryside and villages among the people. He went as far as Caesarea Philippi with its idols and the Gates of Hell, where Gentiles believed demons passed in and out of the world. He traveled through the Ten Towns and stayed in Samaria. And though

I did not follow Him, I pondered His words. "The Kingdom of Heaven is like a merchant on the lookout for choice pearls. When he discovered a pearl of great value, he sold everything he owned, and bought it!" What was this pearl? What did I have to sell to buy it?

As the Law required, He returned to Jerusalem three times each year, for the Festival of Unleavened Bread, the Festival of Harvest, and the Festival of Shelters. And each time Jesus came with His offerings to God, the priests grew more hostile, more determined to turn the people against Him. They even became allies with those they despised, the Herodians, who asked questions that could have caused Him to come into conflict with Roman law.

"Tell us—is it right to pay taxes to Caesar or not?"

In response, Jesus asked for a coin. When given a denarius, He asked the Herodian scribes whose picture and title were on it. Caesar's, of course. "Give to Caesar what belongs to Caesar, and give to God what belongs to God."

Sadducees questioned Him on the resurrection of the dead, and Jesus said they were mistaken in their understanding of Scripture. "God said to Moses, 'I am the God of Abraham, the God of Isaac, and the God of Jacob.' So He is the God of the living, not the dead."

His words astonished me. All Jews knew the bones of the patriarchs lay in the cave of Machpelah near Hebron. And yet, they lived? What He said confused me more than enlightened me. The harder I tried to understand what I had learned, the more confused I became.

The multitudes grumbled. Some said He was a good man; others said He led the people astray. The priests wanted Him seized, but no one dared lay hands on Him. He and His disciples camped on the Mount of Olives, but I didn't go there,

afraid of what others would say if I was seen. So I waited,
knowing Jesus would come early to the Temple.

I was there when some scribes and Pharisees dragged a
half-clad woman before Him. "Teacher," they said, though
I knew the title rankled them, "this woman was caught in
adultery, in the very act. The law of Moses says to stone her.
What do you say?" The trembling woman covered herself as
best she could. She tucked her legs beneath her and covered
her head with her arms. Men stared, whispering, for she was
beautiful. Some sniggered. I moved behind a column and
watched, sickened. I had seen her that morning with one of
the scribes.

Jesus stooped and wrote on the ground. Did He write
that the Law also prescribed the man who shared her bed be
stoned with her? I could not see. When Jesus straightened, I
held my breath, for the Law was clear. The woman must die.
If He told them to let her go, He would break the Mosaic law,
and they would have cause to accuse Him. If He said to stone
her, He usurped the power of Rome, for only the governor
could order execution.

"Let the one who has never sinned throw the first stone."
He stooped and wrote again.

No one dared lift a stone, for only God is sinless. I stayed
behind a pillar to see what Jesus would do. Next He looked
at the woman. "Where are your accusers? Didn't even one
of them condemn you?"

"No, Lord." Tears streaked down her face.

"Neither do I. Go your way. From now on, sin no more."

Though I was touched by His mercy, I wondered. What
of the Law?

I did not follow Him then, though I drank in His words.
Even when many of the leading priests called Him a false

prophet, despising and rejecting Him, He drew me with His teaching.

"A Nazarene carpenter as the Messiah of God! It is blasphemy even to suggest it!"

None of us—not even his closest friends—guessed what Jesus had meant when He said, "When you have lifted up the Son of Man, then you will understand that I Am He."

+   +   +

Near the end of the week, with trepidation, yet full of hope, I went to Jesus. I had met Peter and Andrew and Matthew. I knew John, and he encouraged me: "Speak to the Master." I dared not share my deepest hope with John: to become a disciple, to be worthy enough to travel with Him.

Surely, all my training, all my hard work and self-sacrifice, had prepared me to be counted among His disciples. I thought I could help Him. I had connections, after all. I wanted Jesus to know how hard I had worked all my life to keep the Law. When He knew these things, I expected Him to give me the assurance I wanted. I had much to offer Him. He would welcome me. Or so I thought.

I was a fool!

I will never forget Jesus' eyes as He answered my questions.

I had sought His approval; He exposed my pride and self-deceit. I had hoped to become one of His disciples; He told me what I must give up to become complete. He gave me all the proof I needed to confirm He was the Messiah. He saw into the heart of me, the hidden secrets even I had not suspected were there.

And then Jesus said what I had longed to hear. "Come, follow Me."

I could not answer.

Jesus waited, His eyes filled with love.

He waited.

God waited and I said nothing!

Oh, I believed in Him. I did not understand all He said, but I knew Jesus was the Messiah.

And still, I walked away. I went back to all I knew, back to the life that left me empty.

+   +   +

Months passed. How I suffered, my mind tortured by thoughts of Sheol! When I went up the steps of the Temple, I put coins in the hands of beggars, and cringed inwardly. I knew the truth. I gave not for their sake, but my own. A blessing—that's what I was after! Another mark in my favor, a deed to bring me closer to the assurance of hope and better things to come. For me.

What I had viewed as blessing and God's favor had turned out to be a curse testing my soul. And I had failed, for I had no conviction to give up what gave me honor and position and pleasure. Again and again, I failed. Day after day, week after week, month after month.

I wished I had never heard the name of Jesus! Rather than ease the restlessness of my soul, His words scourged my conscience and tore at my heart. He turned the foundations of my life into rubble.

Passover approached. Jews poured into Jerusalem. I heard Jesus had ridden the colt of a donkey up the road lined by people waving palm fronds and singing, "Praise God for the Son of David! Blessings on the one who comes in the name of the Lord! Praise God in highest heaven!"

Jesus, the Messiah, had come.

I didn't go out to see Him.

When He entered the Temple, He took a whip and drove out the money changers and merchants who filled the court that should have been left open for Gentiles seeking God. He cried out against those who had made His Father's house of prayer into a robbers' den. People scattered before His wrath.

I wasn't there. I heard about it later.

He taught in the Temple every day. His parables exposed the hypocrisy of the religious leaders, fanning their hatred while they pretended not to understand. They twisted His words, trying to use them against Him. They oppressed those who loved Him, even threatening a poor cripple with expulsion from the Temple because he carried his mat after Jesus healed him on the Sabbath.

"Woe to you, scribes and Pharisees, hypocrites!"

I trembled when I heard Him. I hid at His approach.

"Everything you do is for show! On your arms you wear extra wide prayer boxes with Scripture verses inside, and you wear robes with extra long tassels. And you love to sit at the head of the table at banquets and in the seats of honor in the synagogues! *Woe to you!*" His voice thundered and echoed as He strode the corridors of the Temple. "You shamelessly cheat widows out of their property and then pretend to be pious by making long prayers in public."

Scribes shouted against Him, but they could not drown out the truth that poured from His mouth. He indicted the priests, who were to be shepherds of God's people and behaved, instead, like a pack of wolves devouring the flock.

"You take a convert and make him twice the child of hell you yourselves are! Blind guides! Fools! You are careful to tithe even the tiniest income from your herb gardens, but you ignore the more important aspects of the law—justice, mercy, and faith."

The walls of the Temple reverberated at the sound of His voice. The voices of those He confronted sounded as nothing before His wrath. I shook with fear.

"You will never see me again until you say, 'Blessings on the one who comes in the name of the Lord!'"

He left the Temple. Like sheep after the shepherd, His disciples followed. Some looked back in fear, others with excited pride. Voices rose in anger. The scribes and Pharisees, the priests, everyone seemed to be shouting at once. Would the anger inside this place overflow to the streets beyond? Faces twisted in rage. Mouths opened in curses upon the Nazarene. Some tore their clothing.

I fled.

I remember little of what I felt that day other than I had to get away from the wrath inside the Temple. Jesus walked away with His disciples. Part of me wanted to follow; the practical side of me held back. I told myself I had no choice. What Jesus asked of me would dishonor my father. I knew He had not asked the same of others. Why did He demand so much of me?

His words were like a two-edged sword, slicing through the lies I believed about myself. I was not the man of God I thought I was.

And then Jesus turned and looked at me. For the barest moment, I saw the invitation. Did I want to go back inside the Temple to my prayers and quiet contemplation, ignoring all that went on around me? Or did I want to follow a man who looked into me and saw the hidden secrets of my heart? One way required nothing; the other, everything.

I shook my head. He waited. I backed away. I saw the sorrow come into His eyes before He walked away.

I feel that sorrow now. I understand it more today than ever before.

The next time I saw Jesus, He hung on a cross between two thieves at Golgotha. A sign written in Hebrew, Latin, and Greek, hung above his head: "Jesus the Nazarene, the King of the Jews."

I cannot explain what I felt when I saw Jesus outside the city gate, nailed on a Roman cross. Men I knew hurled insults at Him. Even in His hour of suffering and death, they had no pity. I felt anger, disappointment, relief, shame. I justified myself. It seemed I had not turned my back on God after all. I had rejected a false prophet. Hadn't I?

What does that say of me? I thought myself a righteous young man striving always to please and serve God. Jesus exposed me as a fraud. The shame comes back to me now, years later. Such was my arrogance! Such was my willful blindness to the truth! I was equally ashamed of the religious leaders. Men I respected, even revered, stood below the cross, smirking, casting insults, mocking Jesus as He died. They felt no pity, showed no mercy. Not even the wailing of Jesus' mother or the weeping women with her could rouse their compassion.

The rabbi I had followed for so long was among them. They reminded me of vultures tearing at a dying animal.

Would I become like them?

And where were Jesus' disciples? Where were the men who had lived with Him for the past three years, who had left their homes and livelihoods to follow Him? Where were those who had stood along the road waving palm fronds and singing praises as Jesus entered Jerusalem? Had it been less than a week ago?

I remember thinking, *Was it this poor carpenter's fault that we expected so much of Him?* When given the choice between an insurrectionist like Barabbas and a man who spoke of peace with God, the people clamored for the freedom of the one who killed Romans.

Nicodemus stood in the gate, tears streaming down his face, into his beard. Arms crossed, hands shoved deeply into his sleeves, he rocked back and forth, praying. I approached my father's old friend, alarmed to see him in such distress. "May I help you?"

"Be thankful your father did not live to see this day, Silas. They would not listen! They set out to do what they would do. An illegal trial by night, false accusations, false witnesses; they've condemned an innocent man. God, forgive us."

"You are an honest man, Nicodemus." I thought to absolve him. "It is Rome who crucifies Jesus."

"We all crucify Him, Silas." Nicodemus looked up at Jesus. "The Scriptures are being fulfilled even as we stand here watching Jesus die."

I left him to his grief. His words frightened me.

I celebrated Passover as the Law required, but felt no joy in reliving the deliverance of Israel from Egyptian bondage. Jesus' words kept coming back to me. "God blesses those who are poor and realize their need for Him, for the Kingdom of Heaven is theirs."

God had made death pass over His people in Israel. If Jesus was the Messiah, as I had once thought and Nicodemus still believed, what vengeance would God take against us? What hope had we of God's intervention?

I dreamed of Jesus that night. I saw His eyes again, looking at me, waiting as He had that day when He left the Temple.

When I awakened, the city was dark and silent. My heart beat heavily. I felt something in the air.

"I am the way and the truth and the life," Jesus had said. The proclamation of God or words of a madman? I didn't know anymore.

The way was lost, the truth silenced, the hope of the life Jesus offered as dead as He was.

It seemed the end of everything.

+ + +

"YOU have been hard at work for a long time, Silas." Epanetus stood in the doorway. "When we asked you to write your story, we did not intend you to become a slave to it."

Silas put the reed into the pen case and blew on the last few letters he had written. "I've been lost in the past."

"Has it been a comforting journey?"

"Not entirely." He rolled the scroll carefully. His muscles were stiff, his back aching. As he rose, he stretched. "I was deaf and blind."

"And Jesus gave you ears to hear and the eyes to see. Come, my friend. Walk with me in the garden."

The warmth of the sun melted the tension in Silas's shoulders. He filled his lungs with the sea air. Birds flitted about the garden, *ta-ta-whirring* from hidden perches. He felt safe here, as though a thousand miles from Rome, the arena, the maddened, screaming mob, but still not far enough away to escape from the memories of what happened there.

"Where are you in your story?"

"Jesus' death."

"I would give all I own to see His face, even for a moment."

Silas winced inwardly, thinking of the years he'd wasted when he could have been with Jesus.

"What is it you remember most about Jesus?"

"His eyes. When He looked at me, I knew He saw everything."

Epanetus waited for him to say more, but Silas had no intention of satisfying the Roman's curiosity about what *everything* he meant.

"Do you long for Jerusalem, Silas?"

That was an easy enough question to answer. "Sometimes. Not the way it is now. The way it once was." Was that even true? Did he long for the days before Christ came? No. He longed for the *new* Jerusalem, the one Jesus would bring at the end of the ages.

"Do you still have family there?"

"No blood relations, but there may be Christian brothers and sisters still there." Perhaps a few remained firmly rooted, like hyssop in the stone walls of the city. He hoped so, for he prayed continually that his people would repent and embrace their Messiah. "I don't know if anyone remains or not. I only hope. It's been years since I stepped foot in Judea." *May the Lord always call someone to preach there, to keep the gate open for His people to enter into the fold.*

"Perhaps you will go back."

Silas smiled bleakly. "I would prefer God called me to the heavenly Jerusalem."

"He will. Someday. We all pray that your time will not be soon."

Some prayers Silas wished were left unsaid. "Had I remained in Rome, I might be there now." Perhaps he should have stayed.

"God willed you here, Silas."

"The scrolls are precious. They must be safeguarded."
He paused before a fountain, soothed by the sound of
water. "I should be making copies of the scrolls, not writing about my trials."

"We need the testimony of men like you, who walked
with Jesus, who heard His teaching, who saw the miracles."

"I didn't. I told you. My faith came late."

"But you were there."

"In Judea. In Jerusalem. Once in Galilee. In the Temple."

"Write what you remember."

"I remember sorrow. I remember the joy of seeing Christ
risen. I remember my shame and guilt being washed away.
I remember receiving the Holy Spirit. I remember men
who served Christ and died for it. So many I've lost count.
My closest friends are with the Lord, and I feel . . ." He
clenched and unclenched his hands.

"Envy?"

He let out a sharp breath. "You see too clearly, Epanetus." Silas wished he could, for he felt lost in the mire of
his own emotions. "I am so filled with *feelings*, and I fear
none reflect the Spirit of God."

"You are a man, not God."

"A ready excuse I can't accept. Peter hung upside
down upon a cross, dying in agony, and still he prayed for
those who nailed him there! He prayed for every person
in that arena. He prayed the same words our Lord did:
'Father, forgive them.' Forgive the whole wretched mass
of mankind. And what did I pray? For judgment! For their
annihilation! I would have rejoiced to see every Roman
burned by God's fire, and Rome itself made ash!"

He felt Epanetus's silence and thought he understood it.
"Do you still want me under your roof?"

"Roman blood runs in my veins. Do you pray now that God will judge me?"

Silas shut his eyes. "I don't know."

"An honest answer, and I won't put you out for it. Silas, I knew the same kind of bitterness when several of my friends were murdered by zealots in Jerusalem. I hated every Jew in sight and took vengeance whenever allowed. I don't know how many of your people I killed or arrested. And then I met a boy. About Curiatus's age. And he had more wisdom than any man I'd ever known." He laughed softly. "He said he knew the God of all creation, and that same God wanted to know me, too. It was the first time I had heard of Jesus. The miracle was I listened."

"You were wiser than I."

"You came to faith evenutally. That is what matters."

"When were you in Judea?"

His eyes flickered. "Years ago. What a country! Intrigue and savagery are not limited to Rome, my friend. Men are the same everywhere."

"Some men never change. After all these years, I find my faith as frail as it was in the first weeks after Jesus ascended."

"You suffer because you love Him, Silas. You love His people. Love brings suffering. God will help you find your way."

Macombo came out to them. "The brothers and sisters are beginning to arrive."

Silas joined them in prayer and singing praises to Jesus. He closed his eyes and covered his face as Patrobas read Peter's letter. No one asked him to say anything. Even Curiatus remained silent, though he sat close to Silas. Diana was there also. Silas thought of Peter and his wife.

They had teased each other with the familiarity of long years together rich in love.

Diana smiled at him, and his heart quickened.

He had felt euphoria before. And every time it had had to do with Jesus.

He looked at Epanetus talking with Macombo, Urbanus laughing with Patrobas. These people reminded him piercingly of those who had met in the upper room in Jerusalem so many years ago—men, women, slave, free, rich, poor. Jesus brought them all together and made them one family. One in Christ, one body, one Spirit.

The darkness he had felt pressing in around him rolled back a little and gave him a glimpse of the confidence he had lost. Not confidence in himself, but in the One who saved him.

+   +   +

I LAUGH now as I think of it. How can I express the joy I felt on the day I saw Jesus alive again? He looked at me with love, not condemnation! A friend of mine knew where the disciples had hidden, and we went to tell them the good news. We were both shaking with exhaustion and excitement by the time we knocked on the door of the upper room.

We heard voices inside, frightened, arguing. Peter, firmly commanding, "Let them in."

My friend whispered loudly, "Let us in!"

"Who is with you?"

"Silas! A friend of mine. We have news of Jesus!"

Peter opened the door. I could see he did not remember me, and I was glad of it. My friend blurted out, "Jesus lives!"

"He was just here."

My heart raced as we entered. I looked around the room.

I wanted Jesus to know I'd changed my mind. I would do whatever He asked of me now. "Where is He?"

"We don't know. He was here for a while, and then He was gone."

"We were all sitting here and suddenly, there He was."

"It was no ghost," I said. "It was Jesus. We must go to the Temple."

Matthew laughed. "So we can be arrested?"

"I'll go." I was brave in that brief moment.

Peter put his hand on my arm. "Caiaphas and the others will silence you."

"Stay with us," John said.

"We'll leave soon. Come with us to Galilee."

For months, I had wished to be a part of this group of chosen men, but I could not in good conscience leave Jerusalem. "I can't!" How could I go knowing that Jesus was alive? "Others must hear the good news. I must tell Nicodemus."

I knew where to find my father's old friend. Nicodemus saw me coming, and met me in the portico. A finger to his lips, he drew me aside. "I can see by your face the news you bring. Rumors abound."

"It's no rumor, Nicodemus."

"Jesus' body is missing. That does not mean He's come back to life."

I leaned close. "I've seen Him with my own eyes, Nicodemus. He's alive!"

His eyes glowed, but he looked around cautiously. "Unless Jesus walks into the Temple and declares Himself, nothing will change."

"How can you say that? Nothing will ever be the same again."

His fingers dug into my arm as he guided me to the Temple

steps. He spoke low, head down. "Caiaphas and several others met with the Roman guards left in charge of the tomb. They have paid them a large bribe to say Jesus' disciples came during the night while they were sleeping, and stole His body."

"The moment Pontius Pilate hears of this, they will be executed for negligence of duty."

"Lower your voice, my son. The priests will stand up for the guards who have agreed to be part of this plan. Go back to Jesus' disciples. Tell them what Caiaphas and the others have done. They intend to spread this rumor quickly and as far as possible in order to discredit any claims that Jesus lives. Go! Hurry! They must convince Jesus to come to the Temple and declare Himself."

I told Peter what Nicodemus had said, but he shook his head. "None of you must make the same mistake I did. I tried to tell Jesus what to do once. He called me Satan and told me to get away from Him."

"But surely it would make all things clear to Caiaphas and members of the high council if He did go to the Temple."

Simon the Zealot stood. "I heard Jesus say that even if a man returned from the dead, those men would not believe. If Jesus stood before them and showed them His nail-scarred hands and feet, they would still deny He is the Christ, the Son of the living God!"

Seven of Jesus' disciples left for Galilee.

Peter told me later that Jesus had built a fire, cooked fish, and met with the seven disciples on the shores of the Sea of Galilee. He appeared to a crowd of five hundred—I among them—and then to His brother James. For forty days, Jesus walked the earth and spoke with us. I have not the words to tell you the many things I saw Him do, the words He said.

He blessed us, and then He returned to the home from which He came: heaven.

I saw the Lord taken up in a cloud. The disciples and all the rest of us would still be on that mount had not two angels appeared. "Someday He will return from heaven in the same way you saw Him go!"

Oh, how I long for that day to come.

All of them are gone now, those friends I held so dear. Of the 120 who met in the upper room to praise God and pray, the 120 who first received the Holy Spirit who lit our faith on fire, and sent us out to proclaim Him, only two remain: John, the last of the Twelve, whose faith flashes like a beacon from Patmos, and me, the most unworthy.

Every day, I look up and hope I'll see Jesus coming through the clouds.

Every day, I pray *someday* will be today.

THREE

AFTER JESUS *ascended to His Father, those of us who followed Jesus remained in Jerusalem. The Twelve—except for Judas the betrayer, who killed himself—stayed in the upper room, along with others who had come from the district of Galilee, including my friend Cleopas. Mary, Jesus' mother, and His brothers, James, Joseph, Jude, and Simon were there, along with the Lord's sisters and their families, and Mary's sister as well. Nicodemus and Joseph of Arimathea came and went. We prayed for them constantly, for Caiaphas had learned they had taken down Jesus' body, anointed it, and placed it in Joseph's tomb, and he now threatened them with expulsion from the Temple. Mary Magdalene, Joanna, Mary the mother of James the younger, and Salome were also there with us, along with Matthias and Barsabbas, who had followed Jesus from the day John baptized Him in the Jordan River. The Lord chose Matthias to replace Judas as one of the Twelve.*

Fifty days after Jesus had been crucified, forty-seven after He arose, seven days after He ascended to His Father in heaven, on the day of Pentecost, when Jews from all over the empire gathered in Jerusalem, there came upon that house a violent, rushing wind such as I had never heard before or since. It filled the place, and then tongues of fire appeared on each of us. The Holy Spirit filled me, and I felt compelled along with the others to run outside. The fear of men that had haunted us was gone! We rushed headlong into the crowd, crying out the Good News!

A miracle took place inside us. We spoke languages we had not known. Peter spoke before the crowd with eloquence and a knowledge of Scripture that astounded the scribes. Where did a common fisherman come by such wisdom? We know it came from Jesus, poured into him through the Holy Spirit!

I had a gift for languages, but on that day, I spoke to Parthians, Medes, Elamites, and Mesopotamians, all in languages unknown to me until then. That day of miracles, Christ spoke to all men through us. The Lord declared Himself to men and women from Cappadocia, Pontus, Asia, and Phyrgia. The Good News was preached to families from Pamphylia, Egypt, Cyrene, and as far away as Libya and Rome itself! Even Cretans and Arabs heard Jesus was the Savior, Lord of all!

Of course, some did not understand. They scoffed, hearing only babbling and gibberish. Their minds were closed and dark, their hearts hardened to the truth. But thousands heard, and three thousand men accepted Jesus as Savior and Lord. In one day, our little band of 120 believers grew to over three thousand! I've wondered since: was it one language we all spoke? the language all men knew before the Tower of Babel? the language all believers will one day speak in heaven? I know not.

When Pentecost ended, though we did not want to depart from one another, most went home, carrying with them the knowledge that Jesus Christ is the resurrection and the life, Lord of all creation. Later, when I began my travels with Peter and Paul, we found those whose faith had taken root on Pentecost, and begun to grow in a hundred different places.

Those of us who lived in Judea remained in Jerusalem. We were one family, meeting together to hear the apostles teach all Jesus had taught them. We shared meals together, prayed together. No one suffered from need, for we all shared everything we had.

The Lord continued to manifest His power through Peter, who healed a lame man.

Peter, who had once denied Christ three times and hidden with the other disciples out of fear for their lives, now preached boldly in the Temple, along with young John.

The Sadducees and priests, led by Caiaphas and Annas, denied the Resurrection, and put forth lies they had paid the Roman guards to tell. But where was Jesus' body? Where was the proof? In heaven!

The message spread, maddening the high council. The Holy Spirit moved like wildfire through the streets of Jerusalem. Two thousand more soon accepted Christ Jesus as the way, the truth, and the life.

Persecution and suffering came swiftly as Caiaphas and others of like mind tried to put out the fire of faith. Nicodemus and Joseph of Arimathea were expelled from the high council and shunned by religious leaders. Peter and John were arrested. Gamaliel, a righteous man devoted to God, spoke wisely, suggesting the council wait and see if the movement would die on its own. "If this is from God, you will only find yourselves fighting against God." The high council ordered Peter and John flogged before being freed.

We all hoped Gamaliel's advice would sway the leaders. We prayed they would turn to Christ for salvation and join us in worshipping the Messiah we had been praying for centuries would come.

It was not to be. They hardened their hearts against the proof, more afraid of losing their power and prestige than of spending eternity in Sheol, away from the mercy of God.

In truth, I have learned over the years that most men refuse the free gift of salvation through Christ, and continue to believe they can save themselves by their good deeds and adherence to laws and man-made traditions. It is a miracle of God that any are saved at all.

We met every day in the Temple. Smaller groups met in houses throughout the city. Those of us who had the means took in those who lost their homes and livelihoods. God provided. We kept right on teaching and preaching, despite threats and beatings.

All my doubts had been swept away when I saw the risen Jesus; my fears, on Pentecost. I testified out of the joy of my salvation. Every breath was a thanksgiving offering to the Lord who saved me. God had sent His Son, appointed heir of all things, through whom He made the world. Jesus radiates God's own glory, and expresses the very character of God. He sustains everything by the mighty power of His command, proven by His death on the cross and His resurrection. He purified us from sins, and now sits at the right hand of God Almighty. He is King of kings, Lord of lords!

I could not speak enough of Him. I could not spend enough time in the company of those who loved Him as I did. I could not wait to tell the lost sheep: "He is the Christ of God, the Savior of the world, the Shepherd who will lead you home."

+ + +

Perhaps it was due to my ability to write that I was made a member of the first council, for I was certainly not worthy to be counted among them.

"I was his brother and I didn't know Him," James told me when I tried to decline. "I stayed away when He was crucified because I was ashamed of Him. And yet, He came to me and spoke with me after He arose." James became one of the leaders, along with Peter, who had become an immovable rock of faith.

With each week that passed, more came to believe, and the number of gatherings swelled. As our numbers increased, so too did our troubles. The devil is cunning; rousing anger was one of his many weapons. Arguments broke out between Jews who had lived in Judea all their lives and those who came from Greece. The Twelve spent most of their time serving Communion and settling disputes with little time left over to teach what Jesus had taught them. They grew exhausted. Tempers flared, even among the Twelve.

"Jesus sought solitude to pray!" Matthew said. "He needed time to be alone with His Father! Yet I have not a moment to myself!"

Philip groaned. "The only time we're alone is in the middle of the night."

John leaned back. "And by then, I'm too tired to think, let alone pray."

"The Lord always found time." Peter paced. "We must find time as well."

"These people have so many needs!"

James, Jude, and I had discussed the problem at length and prayed about it. We sought to encourage and help if we could, but a solution eluded us.

Then someone said, "How long can we shoulder the whole load ourselves without complete collapse? Even Moses had seventy helpers."

It caused me to think. "A landowner has foremen who hire workers to plow, sow seed, and harvest crops."

"Yes, and an army has a commander who gives orders to his centurions who lead soldiers into battle."

The Twelve huddled together in prayer, and then called all the disciples together. Seven men were to be chosen from among us to serve tables. From that day forward, to the benefit of all, the Twelve devoted themselves to prayer and teaching the Word.

Our meetings were peaceful and joy filled.

But outside, in the city streets, persecution grew worse. The religious leaders said we were a cult drawing the people away from worshipping the Lord in His holy Temple. We met daily in the corridors, and were sometimes driven out. When we preached in the streets, they arrested us. Stephen, one of the seven chosen to serve the church, performed signs and wonders that brought many to believe in Christ. Members of the Synagogue of Freed Slaves argued with him. Failing in that, they lied, and told members of the high council that Stephen spoke blasphemy. Arrested, Stephen was taken before the high council. His words so infuriated the members, they drove him out of the city and stoned him to death.

Grief did not stop the spread of the Good News. Though the apostles remained, persecution drove many believers from Jerusalem, scattering them throughout Judea and Samaria. Like seeds blown by the wind, their witness for Christ was planted everywhere they settled.

The council tried to stifle the message, but the Holy Spirit blazed within us. We went daily to the Temple, to the neighborhood synagogues, and from house to house, teaching and preaching Jesus as the Christ. Philip went to Samaria. When we heard how many came to faith in Christ there, Peter and John went down to help.

I felt no call from God to leave Jerusalem, not even when I was dragged out of my bed in the dead of night and beaten so severely it took months to heal.

"You blaspheme against God by calling Jesus of Nazareth the Messiah!" Six Pharisees smashed every urn, tore down curtains, cut open cushions and poured oil on the Persian carpets while I was accused, beaten, and kicked.

"We should burn this place down so they can't meet here again!"

"If you set fire to this house, it may spread to the street and beyond."

"If you preach one more word about that false messiah, blasphemer, I'll kill you."

I wanted to have the faith of Stephen and ask God's forgiveness for them, but had not the breath to speak. All I could do was look up into my attacker's face.

I had seen him in the Temple among Gamaliel's students. We all learned to dread the name Saul of Tarsus.

+ + +

Over the next months, while I convalesced, serving with reed pen and ink, I heard of Saul's conversion. I gave little credence to the rumors; for I had seen his face so filled with hatred he seemed grotesque. I had felt his heel in my side.

"I heard he met Jesus on the road to Damascus."

I thought immediately of my own experience, but brushed the thought aside. Others said Saul was blind. Some said he still lived in Damascus with a man who accepted Christ as Messiah during Pentecost.

We knew Saul had gone north to Damascus with letters from the high council giving him permission to find all who belonged to the Way, and bring captives bound for judgment back to Jerusalem. Nicodemus and Joseph of Arimathea told us Saul had been with the men who killed Stephen. I wrote letters to warn them of danger and trusted in God to protect His own.

We heard the great persecutor had been baptized. A

report came that Saul was declaring Jesus the Christ in the synagogues of Damascus. Another reported Saul the Pharisee had gone away to Arabia. Why, no one could say.

Men live in hope of their enemies repenting, and Saul of Tarsus had proven what an enemy he was.

I doubted all the reports about Saul's transformation. I hoped never to see his face again.

Joseph, a Levite of Cypriot birth, told me, "Saul is in Jerusalem!" We all called Joseph "Barnabas" because he constantly encouraged everyone in their faith, even those who whined incessantly about their circumstances. "He would like to speak with us."

Ah, Barnabas, the one to always think the best of a man. Even a man like Saul of Tarsus! I remembered being angry at him for the first time. I had not forgotten the night that Pharisee entered my house, nor the weeks of pain I'd suffered until my broken ribs healed. "I don't trust him."

"The Pharisees despise him, Silas. He's in hiding. Did you know priests went up to Damascus to find him, and when they did, he was preaching in a synagogue and declaring Jesus is the Christ? They argued, but he confounded them with proof from the Scriptures. He knows the Torah and Prophets better than anyone."

I grew more stubborn. "The best way to find and kill all of us is to pretend to be one of us, Joseph."

Barnabas studied my face with eyes too much like Jesus'. "Do you hold a grudge against him for what he did to you?"

His words cut deeply, and I answered through gritted teeth. "I have no right to judge any man. None of us do." And then the knife. "But we must be discerning, Joseph. We must see what fruit a tree bears."

Barnabas wasn't fooled. "And how can we see unless we look?"

"You've met him."

"Yes. I've met him. I like him."

"You like everyone. If you met King Herod, you'd like him."

"You're afraid of Saul."

"Yes, I'm afraid of the man. Anyone in their right mind would be afraid of him!"

"I assure you I am in my right mind, Silas, and we must meet with Saul. He is a believer. More zealous than anyone I know."

"Indeed, he's zealous. I saw how zealous. Were you in Damascus?"

"No."

"I'm not as quick as you to believe reports from men I don't know. What if it's all an elaborate plot to hunt down and kill Peter and the rest?"

"Jesus said not to fear death, Silas. Perfect love expels all fear."

Gentle words gently spoken, but a spear to my heart. "Then we know, don't we? My love is not perfect."

His eyes filled with compassion. "Is it fear, Silas, or hatred at the heart of your suspicions?"

Confronted, I confessed. "Both."

"Pray for him, then. You cannot hate a man when you pray for him."

"It depends on the prayer."

He laughed and slapped me on the back.

The council met. Barnabas defended Saul vehemently. His words challenged our faith in God. We should fear no man, only God. And God had received Saul already. Proof was in his changed character, the power of his preaching—both evidence of the Holy Spirit.

Of course, Barnabas turned to me. "What do you think, Silas? Should we trust him?"

Another test of my faith. I wanted to say I was too biased to give an opinion. A coward's way out. Jesus knew the truth, and the Holy Spirit dwelling within me would give me no peace until I repented of my bitterness. "I trust you, Barnabas. If you say Saul of Tarsus believes Jesus is the Christ, then he does."

When the man I hoped never to see again stood before the members of the council, I wondered if he had changed. He no longer dressed in the finery of a Pharisee, but the eyes were the same, dark and bright, and his face full of tension. He looked around the room, straight into the eyes of each man who received him. When his gaze fixed upon me, he frowned. He was trying to remember where he had seen me before. I knew the moment he remembered.

Saul blushed. I stood stunned when his eyes filled with tears. But he surprised me even more. "I beg your forgiveness," he said in a pained voice. I never expected him to speak of that night, certainly not here among these men.

It was the look of shame in his eyes that convicted me most. "I should have forgiven you a long time ago." I rose and stepped toward him. "You are welcome here, Saul of Tarsus."

✦   ✦   ✦

Saul did not remain long in Jerusalem. His zeal got him into trouble with the Greek-speaking Jews who could not defeat him in debate. Barnabas was afraid for him. "They've already tried to kill you more than once! They'll succeed if we stay here."

"If I die, it's God's will." He had changed in faith, but not personality.

"God's will or your own stubbornness?" I asked.

Barnabas spoke up again. "We are not to test the Lord."

Saul's face stiffened. "You misunderstand me."

"Oh?" I met his glare. "Then what do you call it when you put your head into the lion's mouth?" We always seem blind to our own weaknesses, and quick to point out those of others.

We sent him down to Caesarea and put him on a ship back to Tarsus.

The apostles came and went, preaching in other regions. Jesus' brothers and I, along with Prochorus, Nicanor, Timon, Parmenas, and Nicolas, remained in Jerusalem, attending the flock Caiaphas, Annas, and the others were so intent upon destroying. It was a daily struggle, encouraging the discouraged, teaching those new to the faith, and providing for those who were driven from their homes. By the grace of God, no one went hungry and all had a place to live.

Sometimes I long for the months following Pentecost, when Christians met openly in the Temple and in homes throughout the city. We ate together, sang together, and listened eagerly to the apostles' teaching. Joy filled our hearts to overflowing. Our love for one another was evident to everyone. Even those who did not embrace Jesus as Savior and Lord thought well of us! Not Caiaphas, of course. Not the religious leaders who saw Jesus as a threat to their hold on the people.

I did not run from suffering, nor did I run to it. I had seen Jesus on the cross. I saw Him alive several days later. I had no doubt that He was the Son of God, the Messiah, Savior and Lord. If only all Israel would receive Him!

✦   ✦   ✦

Even after several years, even after Philip told an Ethiopian eunuch about Jesus, we did not fully understand that Jesus meant His message for every man and woman, Jew and Gentile. When Peter baptized six Romans in Caesarea, some of us took issue. How could a pantheistic Roman be acceptable to God? Jesus was our Messiah, the One *Israel* had expected for centuries. Jesus was the Jewish Messiah.

What arrogance!

Cleopas reminded me I was a Roman. Offended, I told him it was only because my father had purchased citizenship.

"You were still born a Roman, Silas. And what about Rahab? She wasn't a Hebrew."

"She became one."

And there was the line of my reasoning, for a while at least. Some said these men Peter brought back with him would have to be circumcised before they could become Christians.

Simon the Zealot took one look at Cornelius, a Roman centurion, and flushed to the roots of his black hair. "The Law forbids us to associate with foreigners, Peter, and yet you entered the house of an uncircumcised Roman and ate with him and his family." He pointed. "Surely *this* is not the Lord's will at work here!" He glared at Cornelius who looked back at him with calm humility, his sword still in its scabbard.

Peter stood firm. "Three times the Lord told me, 'Do not call something unclean if God has made it clean.'"

Everyone spoke at once.

"How can these people become one body with us?"

"They know nothing of the Law, nothing of our history."

"Ask the Roman if he knows what *Messiah* means!"

"Anointed One of God," Cornelius said.

Two Jews had come from Caesarea with Cornelius and his family. "This man is highly respected by the Jews in Caesarea. He is devout and fears God, he and all his household. He prays continually and gives generously to the poor."

"I assure you they understand as well as any of us here." Peter told how an angel had come to Cornelius and told him to send for Peter, who was staying in Joppa. "At the same time the angel spoke to Cornelius, the Lord showed me a vision. *Three* times the Lord spoke to me so that I would not go on thinking a man is unclean because of what he eats or whether he has been circumcised. God is not partial. The Scriptures confirm this. Here is the great mystery that has been hidden from us for centuries. The Lord told Abraham he would be a blessing to *many nations*. And this is what the Lord meant. Salvation through Jesus Christ is for all men, everywhere—for Jew *and* Gentile."

Cleopas looked at me and raised his brows. I knew the Scriptures, and felt the conviction of the Holy Spirit.

Peter spread his hands. "Why should we doubt this? Jesus went to the Samaritans, didn't He? He went to the Ten Towns. He granted the request of a Phoenician woman. Why should it surprise us that the Lord has sent the Holy Spirit to a Roman centurion who has prayed and lived to please God?"

The net of grace was cast wider than we imagined.

Peter left Jerusalem and traveled throughout Judea and Galilee and Samaria. The Lord worked mightily through him wherever he went. He healed a paralytic in Lydda, and raised a woman from the dead in Joppa.

Some Christians moved to Phoenicia, Cyprus, and Antioch to get away from the persecution. Soon believers from Cyprus and Cyrene arrived in Antioch and began preaching to Gentiles. We sent Barnabas to investigate. Rather than return, he sent letters instead. "I have witnessed the grace of God here." He stayed to encourage new believers. "Great numbers are coming to Christ. They need sound teaching. I am going to Tarsus to find Saul."

These were hard years of deprivation due to drought. Crops failed from lack of rain. Wheat became expensive. It became increasingly difficult to provide for those who remained in Jerusalem. We managed and asked nothing from nonbelievers, but prayed for God's wisdom in making the best use of our resources.

Barnabas and Saul arrived with a box full of coins from Gentile believers. "Agabus prophesied a famine will come over and affect the entire world."

A Gentile prophesying? We marveled.

"The Christians in Antioch send this money to help their brothers and sisters in Judea."

All of us, Jew and Gentile, were bound together by a love beyond our understanding.

The famine did come, during the reign of Claudius.

+   +   +

Persecution worsened.

King Herod Agrippa arrested several of the apostles. To please the Jews, he ordered James, the brother of John, put to death by sword. When Peter was arrested, we scrambled for information in hope of rescuing him, but learned he had been delivered to four squads of guards and was chained in the lower part of the dungeon beneath the king's palace.

We met in secret at Mary's house, wild with worry. Her son, John Mark, had also gone to Antioch with Barnabas and

Saul. We discussed all kinds of plans, outrageous and hope-less. With so many guards, we knew no one could ever make their way into the prison, free Peter, and get him out alive. Peter was in God's hands, and we could do nothing but pray. This we did, hour after hour, on our knees. We pleaded with God for Peter's life. He was like a father to us all.

The city filled with visitors for Passover. King Herod promised to bring forth Jesus' greatest disciple, "the big fisherman," Peter. We knew if God did not intervene, Peter would be crucified just as Jesus had been.

We prayed that if Peter was crucified, God would raise him like Jesus. Who then could deny Jesus as Messiah, Lord and Savior of the world?

I confess I had no hope of ever seeing him again.

Someone knocked at the door. Whoever it was knew our code. We sent a servant girl to open the gate, but she ran back. "It's Peter."

"You're out of your mind, Rhoda."

"I know his voice."

"How can he be at the gate when he's chained in the dungeon?"

The knock came again, more firmly this time. Cleopas and I went. And there he was, big and bold as ever! Laughing, we opened the door and would have shouted to the others had he not had the presence of mind to quiet us. "They will be looking for me."

What a story he told us! "I was struck awake while sleep-ing between two guards. And there stood an angel of the Lord, right in my cell. It was all alight. The chains fell off my hands and the door opened. And I just sat there." He laughed. "He had to tell me to get up! 'Quick!' he told me. 'Put on your coat and follow me.' I did. Not one guard saw us as we passed by. Not one! He took me to the gate." He spread his arms wide. "And it opened by itself! We went along a street and then the angel vanished. I thought I was dreaming!" He laughed again.

We all laughed. "If you're dreaming, so are we!"

"We must tell the others you're safe, Peter."

"Later," I said. "First we must get him out of Jerusalem before Herod sends soldiers to find him."

Herod did search for him, but when Peter could not be found, he had the two guards crucified in Peter's place on charges of dereliction of duty, and left their bodies to rot on Golgotha.

+   +   +

John Mark returned to Jerusalem, and Mary came to speak to me. Her husband and my father had known each other. "He's ashamed, Silas. He feels like a coward. He won't tell me what happened in Perga. Maybe he'll talk to you."

When I came to the house, he couldn't look me in the eyes. "My mother asked you to come, didn't she?"

"She thought it might be easier for you to talk to me."

He held his head. "I thought I could do it, and I couldn't. I'm as much a coward now as I was the night they arrested Jesus." He looked up at me. "I ran away that night. Did you know? A man grabbed hold of me, and I fought so hard my tunic was torn off. And I ran. I kept on running." He buried his head in his hands. "I guess I'm still running."

"Everyone deserted Him, Mark. I rejected Him, remember? It wasn't until I saw Jesus alive again that I acknowledged Him."

"You don't understand! It was my opportunity to prove my love for Jesus, and I failed. Paul wanted to keep going.

I told Barnabas I'd had enough. Paul scared me to death. I wanted to come home. Not much of a man, am I?"

"Who's Paul?"

"Saul of Tarsus. He's using his Greek name so they will listen to him." He stood up and paced. "He's not afraid of anyone! When we were in Paphos, the governor, Sergius Paulus, had a magician, a Jew named Elymas. He had the governor's ear and caused us all kinds of trouble. I thought we'd be arrested and thrown in prison. I wanted to leave, but Paul wouldn't hear of it. He said we had to go back. He wouldn't listen to reason."

"What happened?"

"He called Elymas a fraud! He was, of course, but to say it there in the governor's court? And he didn't stop there. He said Elymas was full of deceit and the son of the devil. And there was Elymas, calling down curses on us, and Sergius Paulus's face was turning redder and redder." He paced back and forth. "He signaled the guards, and I thought, *This is it. This is where I die.* And there's Paul, pointing at Elymas and telling him the hand of the Lord was upon him and he'd be blind. And suddenly he was. The guards backed away from us. Elymas flailed around, crying for help." John Mark paused. "The governor went so white I thought he'd die. But then he listened to Paul. He was too afraid not to listen."

John Mark flung his arms high in frustration. "He even ordered a banquet, and Paul and Barnabas spent the whole night talking to him about Jesus and how he could be saved from his sins. But all I wanted to do was get out of there and come home!"

"Did Sergius Paulus believe?"

John Mark shrugged. "I don't know. He was amazed. Whether that means he believed, only the Lord knows." He snorted. "Maybe he thought Paul was a better magician than Elymas."

"How did you get home?"

He sat and hunched his shoulders again. "We put out to sea from Paphos. When we arrived in Perga, I asked Barnabas for enough money to get home. He tried to talk me out of leaving. . . ."

"And Paul?"

"He just looked at me." John Mark's eyes filled with tears. "He thinks I have no faith."

"Did he say that?"

"He didn't have to say it, Silas!" Folding his arms on his knees, he bowed his head. "I have faith!" His shoulders shook. "I do!" He looked up, angry in his own defense. "Just not the kind to do what he's doing. I can't debate in the synagogues or talk to crowds of people I've never met. Paul speaks fluent Greek like you do, but I stumble around when people start asking questions. I can't think fast enough to recite the prophesies in Hebrew let alone another language!" He looked miserable. "Then later, I think of all the things I could have said, things I should have said. But it's too late."

"There are other ways to serve the Lord, Mark."

"Tell me one thing I can do, one thing that will make a difference to anyone!"

"You spent three years following Jesus and the disciples. You were at the garden of Gethsemane the night Jesus was arrested. Write what you saw and heard." I put my hand on his shoulder. "You can sit and think about all that, then write it down. Tell everyone what Jesus did for the people, the miracles you saw happen."

"You're the writer."

"You were there. I wasn't. Your eyewitness account will

encourage others to believe the truth—that Jesus is the Lord. He is God with us."

John Mark grew wistful. "Jesus said He came not to be served, but to serve others and to give His life as a ransom for many."

The young man's countenance transformed when he spoke of Jesus. He relaxed into the firsthand knowledge he had of the Lord. No one would ever doubt John Mark's love for Jesus, nor the peace given to him through his relationship with Him.

"Write what you know so that others can come to know Him also."

"I can do that, Silas, but I want to do the other, too. I don't want to run and hide anymore. I want to tell people about Jesus, people who never even imagined such a God as He is. I just don't feel . . . prepared."

I knew one day Mark would stand steady before crowds and speak boldly of Jesus as Lord and Savior of all. And I told him so. God would use his eager servant's heart. He had spent his life in synagogues and at the feet of rabbis, as I had. But his training had not extended into the marketplaces or gone so far as Caesarea and beyond.

"If you want to go out among the Gentiles to preach, Mark, you must do more than speak their language. You must learn to *think* in Greek. It must become as natural to you as Aramaic and Hebrew."

"Can you help me?"

"From this day forward, we will speak Greek to one another."

And so we did, though his mother grimaced every time she heard her son speak the language of uncircumcised, pagan Gentiles.

"I know; I know," she said after questioning my wisdom on the matter. "If they understand who Jesus is and accept Him as Savior and Lord, then they will no longer be *goyim*; they will be Christians." Sometimes the old prejudices rose to challenge our faith in Jesus' teaching.

John Mark joined us. "In the eyes of Caiaphas and the rest, Mother, we are as *goyim* as the Greeks and Romans."

"You were listening at the door."

"Your voice carries. The old has passed away, Mother. Christians have no barriers of race, culture, or class between them."

"I know this in my head, but sometimes my heart is slow to follow." She reached up and put her hands on his shoulders. He leaned down to receive her kiss. "Go with my blessing." She waved her hand at both of us.

+   +   +

Paul and Barnabas wrote letters from Antioch of Pisidia, where they preached in the synagogues. Some Jews listened and believed; many did not. A few incited the influential religious women and city leaders, and caused a riot. Paul and Barnabas were driven from the town.

"Everywhere we go, certain Jews follow, determined to stop us from preaching Christ as Messiah in the synagogues. . . ."

Even when they went on to Iconium and preached to Gentiles, these enemies came to poison minds against the message. As always, Paul dug in his heels. "We will stay here as long as God allows and preach Christ crucified, buried, and arisen."

They stayed a long time in Iconium, until Jews and Gentiles banded together in a plot to stone Paul. They escaped to Lystra and then to Derbe. Despite the risks, they continued to preach. They healed a man born a cripple in Lystra, and the Greeks thought they were gods. Paul and Barnabas tried to restrain the crowd from worshipping them, and Jews from Antioch used the opportunity to turn the mob against them.

"Paul was stoned by the mob," Barnabas wrote. "The Jews from Antioch dragged his body outside the city gate and dumped him there. We all went out and gathered around him and prayed. When the Lord raised him, our fear and despair lifted. Neither Jew nor Gentile dared touch Paul when we went back into the city. The Lord is glorified! Friends ministered to Paul's wounds, and then we traveled to Derbe and preached there before returning to Lystra to strengthen believers, appoint elders, and encourage our brothers and sisters to hold firmly to their faith when persecution comes. . . ."

Another letter arrived from Pamphylia. They preached in Perga and Attalia. Others wrote as well. "Paul and Barnabas returned by ship to Antioch of Syria. . . ."

The reports encouraged us in Jerusalem.

But troubles arose. False teaching crept in when disciples moved on. Returning to Antioch, Paul and Barnabas discovered trouble that threatened the faith of Gentiles and Jews alike. They came to Jerusalem to discuss the question already causing dissension between Jewish and Gentile brothers.

"Some Jewish Christians are teaching circumcision is required of Gentiles for salvation."

Every member of the church council in Jerusalem had been born a Jew and followed the Law all his life. All had been circumcised eight days after birth. All had lived under the sacrificial system established by God. Even in the light

of Christ crucified and risen, it was difficult to shed the laws
by which we had been reared.

"It is a sign of the covenant!"

"The old covenant!" Paul argued. "We are saved by grace.
If we demand these Gentiles be circumcised, we're turning
back to the Law which we've never been able to keep. Christ
freed us from the weight of it!"

None of us on the council could boast Paul's heritage. Born
a Jew, son of the tribe of Benjamin, a Pharisee and celebrated
student of Gamaliel, he had lived in strictest obedience to the
law of our fathers, his zeal proven in his brutal persecution
of us before Jesus confronted him on the road to Damascus.
Yet, here Paul stood, debating fiercely *against* placing the
yoke of the Law upon Gentile Christians!

"It is false teaching, my brothers! The Holy Spirit has
already manifested Himself in the faith of these Gentiles.
Don't forget Cornelius!" Everyone looked at Peter, who was
nodding thoughtfully.

Paul and Barnabas reported signs and wonders that had
occurred among the Greeks in Lystra, Derbe, and Iconium.

"Surely these events are proof enough of God's acceptance
of them as His children." Paul grew passionate. "God accepts
them. How can we even consider going back to the Law from
which Christ freed us? This cannot be!"

We asked Paul and Barnabas to withdraw so that we could
pray on the matter and discuss it further. His eyes blazed,
but he said no more. He told me later he wanted to argue
the case further, but knew the Lord was training him in
patience. How I laughed over that.

It was not an easy matter for us to decide. We were all
Jews with the law of Moses ingrained in our minds from
childhood. But Peter spoke for all of us when he said, "We

are all saved the same way, by the undeserved grace of the Lord Jesus." Still there were other concerns to address, reasons why some direction must be given these new Gentile Christians so that they wouldn't be easily enticed back into the licentious worship of their culture. I had traveled more widely than most of those on the council and could speak of the issues with personal knowledge. I had seen pagan practices, and so had my father, who had traveled to Asia, Thrace, Macedonia, and Achaia and told me what he saw. We could not just say we are all saved by grace, and not say more!

James spoke for compromise.

While the council discussed the issues, I acted as secretary and made a list of the most important points on which we agreed. We needed to reassure the Gentile Christians of salvation through the grace of our Lord Jesus and encourage them to abstain from eating food offered to idols, engaging in sexual immorality, eating meat from strangled animals, and consuming blood—all things they may have practiced while worshipping false gods. They all agreed that James and I should draft the letter.

"Someone must carry it north to Antioch so that none there can say that Paul or Barnabas have written it."

James was needed in Jerusalem. Judas (also called Barsabbas) volunteered, and then suggested me as his companion.

Peter agreed. "Since the letter will be written by your hand, Silas, you should go and testify to it. Then there will be no question of its origin."

Oh, how my heart beat with excitement. And dread. It had been over ten years since I had ventured outside the boundaries of Judea.

It was time I did.

✦   ✦   ✦

As I prepared for the journey with Judas, Paul, and Barnabas, John Mark came to see me. His Greek was greatly improved, as was his confidence, and he believed strongly that the Lord was calling him back to Syria and Pamphylia. He asked me to speak to Paul on his behalf, which I agreed to do.

I did not expect so firm a refusal from a man who argued so passionately for grace!

"Let him stay in Jerusalem and serve! He was called once before and turned his back on the Lord."

"Called, Paul, but not fully prepared."

"We haven't time to coddle him, Silas."

"He doesn't ask it of you."

"And how long would it be before he missed his mother again?"

His sarcasm grated. "He had reasons other than missing his family, Paul."

"None that convince me he is trustworthy."

I left the matter then, determined to take it up again the next day when he'd had time to think more on the matter. Barnabas tried to warn me.

"It is a sin to hold a grudge, Barnabas." We are so swift to see the faults in others, failing to see the same fault in ourselves.

"It's his determination to spread the message of Christ that presses him on like no other man I know. Paul cannot understand other men who are not so driven as he."

Ignoring his wise advice, I tried again. I thought to go to the heart of the matter.

"You spoke eloquently of grace, Paul. Can you offer none to John Mark?"

"I forgave him."

His tone rankled. "How kind of you."

How easily we forget that harsh words serve only to fan anger into flame.

Paul looked at me, eyes dark, cheeks flushed. "He deserted us in Perga! I can forgive him, but I cannot afford to forget his cowardice."

"John Mark is no coward!"

"I would have more respect for him if he spoke for himself!"

All I had done was make matters worse.

+ + +

Immediately upon our arrival in Antioch of Syria, I read the letter to the congregation. The Gentile Christians were relieved by the instructions of the Jerusalem council, while some Jewish Christians protested. When the seed of pride takes root, it is hard to dig out. Judas and I stayed to teach Christ's message of grace to all who had faith in His crucifixion, burial, and resurrection. A few Jews left, rather than hear more. We continued to encourage those who had not been deceived by men's pride in their own good works. We hoped to strengthen their faith so that they could stand firmly against the persecution we knew would come.

Often, I heard Paul preach. He was a great orator who presented the message with proof from Scripture. He could switch from Greek to Aramaic with ease. He never surrendered when debated, but used his considerable intellect to win converts—or rouse an angry mob! No question confounded him.

I began to understand John Mark's difficulty. A man with

Paul's dramatic conversion experience, intellectual powers, and education could make the most earnest Christian feel ill equipped to serve beside him. If not for the advantages given me in my youth, I too might have been intimidated. I was not afraid of Paul, but his impassioned character and his confidence that he was always right annoyed me on numerous occasions. That he *was* right gained my respect if not affection. Brotherly affection developed through longer acquaintance.

A letter came from Jerusalem.

Paul watched me read the scroll. "What's wrong?"

"Nothing is wrong." I rolled it again, wondering why I felt such deep disappointment to be called home. "Judas and I are called back to Jerusalem."

"Once matters are settled there, come back to Antioch."

His command surprised me. We had said little to each other since our argument over John Mark. While we respected each other, shared faith in Jesus, there remained a barrier between us that neither of us had made great efforts to tear down.

"You are a fine teacher, Silas."

I raised my brows at the compliment and inclined my head. "As are you, Paul." I did not flatter him. "I've never heard a man argue the case for Christ so thoroughly. If faith came through reason, the whole world would accept Jesus as Lord."

"We must do as Jesus commanded! We must go out into all the nations and make disciples!"

"And so you and Barnabas shall." I smiled faintly. "And others." I meant John Mark.

"You are well equipped to do the work, Silas. The council has twelve members, and they can draw from others who knew Jesus personally and walked with Him during those three years He preached. Let the council cast lots for another to replace you."

A man likes to think himself indispensable. "I would not presume—"

"Is it presumption to ask God's will in the matter? I could see it in your face when you read that letter you're holding. You prefer teaching to administration."

"I know more of administration than I do of teaching."

"When we delight in the Lord, He gives us the desire of our hearts. The Scriptures tell us that. And your desire is to go out into the world and preach. Can you deny that?"

"We each have our place in the body of Christ, Paul. I must serve where I'm needed."

He started to say more and then pressed his lips together. With a shake of his head, he spread his hands and walked away.

Judas and I returned to Jerusalem and the council. I spoke with John Mark and saw his disappointment. "I will go to Antioch and speak to Paul myself. Perhaps after we talk, he will see I've lost my timidity."

I thought that a wise idea. The young man was Barnabas's cousin, and Barnabas would encourage Paul to give him a second chance. As for my desire to return to Antioch, I left it to the Lord. I knew there were others who could travel with Paul, men wiser than I in how to deal with his strong personality. But I wanted to go. He challenged my faith. One could not be complacent in his company.

Not long after John Mark left Jerusalem, a letter came from Antioch addressed to Peter and James.

"Silas, Paul asks that you be released from the council so that you can travel with him throughout Syria and Cilicia.

He wants to visit the churches he started and see how they're doing."

The request surprised me. "What of Barnabas? Has he fallen ill?"

"He and John Mark have gone to Cyprus."

I could imagine what had happened between Paul and Barnabas. Paul had not relented, and Barnabas could not crush the spirit of his cousin. Nor should he.

Peter looked at me. "Did Paul speak with you about this while you were in Antioch?"

"Yes." I could feel the others staring. "I told Paul I would serve wherever I'm needed."

James studied my face. "You have been praying about this for some time, haven't you?"

"Unceasingly."

The council members discussed the matter. Some did not want me to leave Jerusalem. My administrative abilities had been of use in the church. But I knew Paul was right. Others could take my place—men of strong character and faith who stood firm despite persecution.

"You've traveled far more than any man here, Silas. You would be a good companion to Paul. Do you feel the Lord calling you to this work?"

"Yes." I had asked the Lord to give me clear opportunity if that was His will, and Paul's letter and the council's response eliminated my doubts.

Other questions would have to wait until I met Paul in Antioch.

We prayed and cast lots. Barsabbas was chosen to take my place. He was an honest, hardworking man who had proven his love of Jesus and the church on many occasions.

I left the next morning for Antioch.

+   +   +

Paul's greeting was cool. "You sent him, didn't you?"

I didn't have to ask whom he meant. His face said it all. Would his anger run so deep we would be unable to work together?

"John Mark told me he intended to speak to you. He thought once you talked with him, you would see he is no longer as timid as he was. I take it things did not go well between you."

"Well enough for others, but I didn't want him on this trip."

By *others*, he meant Barnabas.

"Why not?"

"I have no way of knowing how long we will be gone, Silas. A year at the least, probably longer. I'm not convinced of his dedication."

"And Barnabas disagreed."

"It was the first time I've seen him angry. He insisted Mark go with us. I refused to take the risk."

I smiled faintly. "How do you know I'll have the courage to stay the course?"

A muscle worked near his right eye. "The night I broke down your door, had you beaten, and smashed everything we could lay hands on, you didn't curse me—not once—nor did you cry out against what I was doing." He met my gaze. "I intended to kill you, but your manner stayed my hand."

"*God* stayed your hand."

"I wish He had stayed my hand on other occasions."

I knew he meant his part in the stoning of Stephen. "Our past is the burden we left at the cross." I told him what I had done so there would be no secrets between us.

"At least . . . you never committed murder."

I could not help but smile. "I can see clearly you're an ambitious man, Paul, but let's not compete over who is the greater sinner!"

He looked surprised and then paled. "No! We all have sinned and fallen short of God's glorious standard. This is the truth men need to know so that they will understand their need of our Savior, Jesus Christ."

His anguished declaration told me that the training of a Pharisee continued to test his faith. He had great regret. But didn't we all feel remorse over things of the past—our blindness, the wasted days and years we did not live for Christ? We must remind one another: by grace we are saved, not by works. "There is no condemnation for those who belong to Christ Jesus." Paul would need to be reminded of his own words—often. "God saved us by His grace when we believed. And we can't take credit for this; it is a gift from God." God had chosen this man to bear testimony, and his violent, self-righteous past was proof of God's ability to change a man into a new creation and set him upon a new course.

His eyes grew bright with tears. "We've been washed in His blood."

"And clothed in His righteousness."

"Amen!" We said in unison. We laughed with the joy of free men joined in common purpose.

Paul grasped my arms. "We will do well together, my friend."

Yes, we would, though neither of us knew yet how difficult our days together would be.

FOUR

BEFORE *we began our travels, Paul and I discussed our strategy. "The Greeks know nothing of the Scriptures," he said, "so we must speak to them in ways they will understand."*

My father had said the same thing in several ways. "My father insisted I have training in logic and Greek poetry." I had to know how to think like the Greeks in order to best them in trade.

We would not burden the fledgling congregations with our support. I had some resources on which we could depend, but Paul insisted he would work for a living.

"Doing what?"

"I come from a family of tentmakers. What can you do?"

"I can translate and write letters."

We decided to stay to the major trade routes and centers so the message would have the best chance of being carried more quickly through the empire. We would start with the synagogues. There we expected to be welcomed as travelers and given lodgings as well as the opportunity to preach. We agreed to maintain contact with the Jerusalem council through letters and messengers.

"Even if the Jews welcome the Good News, we must not neglect preaching to the Gentiles in the agoras."

The marketplace was the center of all social, political, and administrative functions in every city from Jerusalem to Rome, and as such would afford us greater opportunity to meet men and women unfamiliar with the news we carried.

Once we made our plans, we set out, visiting the churches in Syria as we headed north. It was hard going. I was not used to traveling on foot. Every muscle in my body ached, each day adding to my discomfort, but Paul was driven, and so drove me as well. I did not protest, for we both thought time short and that Jesus would return soon. I knew I was not so old that my body would not become accustomed to the hardship of travel. We carried in our hearts the most important message in the world: the way of salvation for mankind. Discomfort would not delay us.

Though robbers did.

We were set upon by six men as we traveled north through the Taurus Mountains. When they surrounded us, I wondered if Paul and I would ever make it to Issus or Tarsus. One robber held a knife to my throat while another searched me. Two others dug around in Paul's clothing to find something of value. I should not have been surprised that he carried nothing. He had said from the first day that he would trust in God to provide for us. I was not so mature in my faith, though I had been a believer longer than Paul. I had a pouch of coins tucked into my sash, which a brigand found almost immediately. Other than my coat, a sash my father gave me, the inkhorn and pen case containing reeds, and a small knife for erasures and cutting papyrus, I had nothing of value.

"Look at this!" The robber held up my money pouch and shook it. He tossed it to the leader, who opened it and spilled the denarii into the palm of his hand. He grinned, for it was not a small amount, but enough to carry us for many weeks.

Another searched Paul. "Nothing!" He thrust Paul away in disgust.

"I may not have money," Paul said boldly, "but I have something of far greater value!"

"And what would that be?"

"The way to your salvation!"

They hooted in laughter. One of them stepped forward and put his blade against Paul's throat. "And what about yours, you fool?"

Paul's face flushed. "Even thieves and robbers are welcome at the Lord's table, *if* they repent."

I could see how little they welcomed that declaration, and I prayed our journey would not end with our throats slit on a dusty mountain road. If that was to be our end, I decided not to go silently to the grave. "Jesus died for all our sins—yours as well as mine."

"Who's Jesus?"

I told them everything in short order, while praying that my words would fall like seeds onto good soil. Perhaps their hard lives had plowed the ground and made it ready for sowing. "I saw Him crucified, and met Him four days later. He spoke to me. He broke bread with me. I saw His nail-scarred hands."

"He confronted me on the road to Damascus months later," Paul said, undaunted by the knife at his throat. He gripped the man's wrist and looked at him. "If you leave me dead on this road, know that I forgive you." He spoke with such sincerity, the man could only stare. Paul let go of him. "I beseech the Lord not to hold your sins against you."

"Let him go!" The leader growled.

The robber withdrew, confused.

"Here!" The leader flung the pouch of coins. I caught it against my chest.

"What are you doing?" The others protested. "We need that money!"

"Would you have their god on our heels? Others will come along this road."

Did I trust in God's provision or not? "Keep it!" I tossed the pouch back. "Consider it a gift from the Lord we serve.

Better to accept it than rob others and bring further sin upon yourselves."

"You should be careful what you say." A robber held up his knife.

"The Lord sees what you do." Paul stepped forward, and looked up at the man on horseback. "These men follow in your steps."

He shifted uneasily upon his horse and held my money pouch like a poisonous snake.

"The next band will be sorely disappointed in how little these men have to offer."

I felt encouraged by the robber's sudden concern for our well-being. Fear of the Lord is the foundation of true knowledge. However, his next words filled me with misgivings. "Bring them along!"

They took us into the mountains. Their camp reminded me of En-gedi, where David had hidden in the wilderness from King Saul and his army. Plenty of water, cliff walls for protection, a few women and children to greet them. I was exhausted. Paul talked all night and baptized two of the robbers on the third day of our captivity.

They accompanied us as far as the mountain pass called the Cilician Gates.

"Jubal said to give this to you." The man tossed me the pouch of coins.

God had brought us safely through the mountains. The Cilician plain spread out before us, lush green from the waters of the Cyndnus.

✦   ✦   ✦

We stayed with Paul's family in Tarsus and preached in the synagogues. Paul had come here after meeting the Lord on the

Damascus road and spent time in seclusion before he began preaching the message of Christ. The seeds he had planted had taken root and flourished. The Jews received us with joy.

We moved on to Derbe, a city in Lycaonia, named after the junipers that grew in the area. Again, we preached in the synagogues, and met Gaius, who became a good friend and, later, a traveling companion to Paul. Gaius knew the Scriptures well and embraced the Good News before anyone else.

Lystra filled me with dread. The last time Paul had preached in the Roman colony near the unsettled southern mountains, he had been stoned.

"God raised me," Paul said. "I walked back into the city on my own two legs. Friends washed my wounds and helped me escape with Barnabas." He laughed. "I guess they feared if I remained, my enemies would kill me *again*."

I didn't think it amusing. But I was curious. How many men have died and lived again to tell of it? I asked him what he remembered, if anything.

"I can't say what I saw. Whether my soul left my body or was still in my body, I don't know. Only God knows what really happened, but I was caught up somehow to the third heaven."

"Did you see Jesus?"

"I saw the heavenly realm and earth and all beneath it."

In awe, I pressed. "Did the Lord speak to you?"

"He said what He said to me before. I cannot describe what I saw, Silas, but I was in a state of misery when I came back. That I remember quite well." He smiled wistfully. "The only one who could understand what I felt is Lazarus." He put his hand on my arm, his expression intense. "It is better that we don't speak of the experience, Silas. Those in Lystra know something of it, but I dare not add more."

"Why not?" It seemed to me his experience confirmed our lives continued after our bodies rested.

"People are likely to become more interested in heavenly realms and angels than in making a decision about where they stand with Jesus Christ *in this life*."

As I have said, Paul had more wisdom than I.

I wanted to ask more, to press him for everything he remembered, but I respected his decision. And I did not want to make assumptions about his course of action regarding Lystra. "Those who sought your death would be confounded if they were to face you now." Whether we passed through Lystra or remained to preach was for him to decide. I knew God would make His will known to Paul. The man never ceased to pray for His guidance.

"They *will* be confounded. Whether they listen and believe this time remains to be seen."

Lystra is a Latin-speaking Roman colony in the consolidated province of Galatia. Remote and filled with superstition, it proved hard ground for the seed we bore. But our time there yielded a few tender shoots. And we met one who was to grow tall and strong in faith; a young man named Timothy. His mother, Eunice, and grandmother, Lois, believed in God. His father, however, was a Greek pagan who remained devoted to idol worship.

Eunice came to me and asked to speak with me alone. "I'm afraid to speak to Paul," she confessed. "He is so fierce."

"What troubles you?"

"My son is loved by many, Silas, but as you have probably guessed, he is not a true Jew." She lowered her eyes. "I took him to the rabbi when he was eight days old, but he would not circumcise him because of his mixed blood. And he's never been allowed to enter the synagogue." She worried her shawl. "I was young and headstrong. I married Julius against my father's wishes. I have many regrets, Silas." She lifted her head, eyes moist. "But having Timothy is not one of them. He has been the greatest blessing of my life and my mother's."

"He is a fine boy."

"We saw Paul when he came before. When he was stoned . . ." She clasped her hands tensely. "My son could talk of nothing else after Paul left. He said if Paul ever came back he would follow him anywhere. And now Paul is here again, and Timothy has such hope." Her eyes welled. "Paul is a Pharisee, a student of the great Gamaliel. What will he say when Timothy approaches him? I cannot bear to see my boy crushed again, Silas. I cannot."

I put my hand on her shoulder. "He won't be."

Paul, who had no wife or children of his own, loved this young man like a son. "His mother and grandmother have taught him well. He has a quick mind and an open heart to the Lord. See how he drinks in the Word of God, Silas. He will be of great use to God."

I agreed, but was concerned. "In time, Paul, but he's only thirteen and reserved by nature." I feared that Timothy might prove to be like John Mark, too young to be taken from his family.

"He thinks before he speaks."

"He's somewhat timid in a crowd."

"What better way for him to outgrow those tendencies than to join us in carrying the message to other cities? He will learn to be bold among strangers."

A pity Paul had not encouraged John Mark in this way, but I did not mention this. Both young men had similar traits, though Paul seemed determined not to notice. "Timothy might grow even more timid if persecuted." What Eunice had told me was also heavily on my mind, but I did not know how much to divulge to Paul without causing her embarrassment.

Paul gave me a level look. "He is younger than John Mark, but stronger in faith."

That sarcasm again. I felt the heat rush into my face, and held my tongue with difficulty. Any time anyone argued with Paul, he engaged his considerable talents at debate. In this case, it would serve no other purpose than to pour salt on old wounds. Both of us would suffer in an argument over John Mark.

A few hours later, Paul said, "Perhaps I am unfair."

Perhaps? "John Mark made good use of his time in Jerusalem."

Paul said nothing for a while, but I could see our difference of opinion plagued him. "Persecution will come whether Timothy stays here or goes with us," he said finally. "He might be safer with us than left behind. Besides, we already have leaders in place here, Silas. Timothy can be of much more use elsewhere."

I knew I must voice my other concerns. "As fine a young man as he is, Paul, he will cause us nothing but trouble. You were a Pharisee. You know as well as I do that no Jew will listen to him. No matter how fine his reputation here, everywhere else he will be seen as a Gentile because of his father. Timothy is uncircumcised and, therefore, unclean in their eyes. We both agreed we must meet people and speak to them in ways they will understand. How can he go with us? He won't be allowed in the synagogues! You know as well as I if we try to take him inside with us, there'll be a riot. The Good News won't be heard at all with Timothy as our traveling companion. Let him cut his teeth teaching Gentiles here."

Paul chewed on his lip, eyes narrowed in thought. "I think we should lay the matter before Timothy and see what he says about it."

Timothy presented the solution. "Circumcise me. Then no one can protest my presence in the synagogue."

The boy's courage and willingness to eliminate any obstacles served to gain my full support in taking him with us. Paul made all the arrangements, and a week later, when Timothy's fever abated and he was well enough to travel, we gathered the church elders from Lystra and Iconium. We all laid hands on Timothy and prayed the Holy Spirit would give him the gift of prophecy and leadership. His mother and grandmother both wept.

I could see how difficult this parting was for the two women. Together, they had raised Timothy to please God, and now they presented him to God as their thanksgiving offering to Jesus Christ. Timothy had been their comfort and joy. Their love of the Lord and the Torah had prepared the way for them all to believe the Good News.

"God will send you where He wills, my son."

Timothy stood tall. "Tell Father I will continue to pray for him." His voice choked with emotion.

"As will we." Eunice laid her hand against his cheek. "Perhaps his love for you will open his heart one day."

We all hoped. And prayed.

✦   ✦   ✦

The three of us traveled from town to town. We spent long hours around campfires talking about Jesus. I told Timothy all I knew, amazed that the memories of Jesus' teachings were so clear—proof that the Holy Spirit refreshed my mind. Paul and I preached whenever and wherever allowed. Timothy did as well, though he would sometimes be so tense and nervous, he would vomit before we approached the synagogue. I saw him sick many times while we worked together in Corinth, and later heard from Paul that even after years in ministry, Timothy still suffered greatly from a nervous stomach. Much of this I'm sure was due to his love for his flock in Ephesus. Timothy always agonized over the people in his care, even those who were wolves among the sheep.

But I digress.

In the beginning, we had Timothy stand with us, a silent encourager, speaking only when questioned directly. When he did speak, he revealed the remarkable wisdom God had given him. He was especially useful in reaching the younger people. While children were sometimes frightened by Paul's passion and put off by my grave dignity, they flocked to Timothy. The boys thought him brave and adventurous; the girls thought him handsome. I laughed when I saw how they surrounded him, first out of curiosity, later out of fond regard.

Paul worried. "It is no laughing matter, Silas. With such admiration comes temptation and sin." He spent a great deal of time instructing Timothy on how to stay pure and avoid temptation.

"Think of the younger ones as your sisters."

"And the older ones?"

"Older ones?" Paul blanched. He looked at me.

I nodded. I had seen more than one young woman approach Timothy with the clear intent of seducing him. "Never be alone with a woman, Timothy. Young or old. Woman is temptation for a man. Treat the older ones with the respect you would show your mother and grandmother."

Paul continued to stare at me. "Was there more you wanted to say?"

"No."

He took me aside later. "I never thought to ask if you had difficulty with women."

I laughed. "All men have difficulty with women, Paul. In some manner or form. But be assured. I take my own advice."

"It is a pity he's so good-looking."

The boy's beauty was a gift from God. As far as I know, Timothy heeded our instructions. I have never heard a word of doubt regarding his integrity.

--------------------------- +   +   + ---------------------------

SILAS put his reed pen in its case and sat thinking of Diana. Every time she looked at him, he felt a catch in his breath and a tightening in his stomach. Was this what it was like to fall in love with someone? How could he love her after such short acquaintance? And the boy, Curiatus . . . He felt drawn to him as Paul had felt drawn to Timothy. The woman and boy made Silas wonder what it might have been like to marry and have children of his own, a son to bring up for the Lord.

Many of the disciples had wives and children. Peter's sons remained in Galilee. His daughter had married, had children, and gone with her husband to another province.

Paul had been adamant about remaining unmarried, and encouraged others to follow his example. "We should remain as we were when God first called us. I had no wife when Jesus chose me to be His instrument, and will never take one. Nor should you, Silas. Our loyalties must not be divided."

Silas had not agreed with him. "Peter's wife has never been a distraction to his love of Christ or his dedication to serving the Master. She shares his faith. She walks the roads with him. She is a great comfort to him when he's weary. And Priscilla and Aquila—look at all they have accomplished. They are yoked together with Christ."

"Peter was married when he met Jesus! So were Priscilla and Aquila."

"God had said, 'It is not good for man to be alone.'"

Aggravated, Paul had glared at him. "Is there a woman you want to make your wife? Is that the point of this argument?"

Silas wanted to pound his fists in frustration. "No."

"Then why are we having this discussion?"

"Not all men are called to be celibate, Paul." Silas spoke quietly, but with firmness. "You don't hear yourself, but sometimes you speak as though celibacy is a new law within the church."

Paul opened his mouth to retort. Uttering an exasperated snort, he surged to his feet and left the fire. He stood out in the darkness looking up at the stars. After a long while, he came back. "Who are we talking about?"

Silas named two couples who had approached him on the subject.

"They're young. Their feelings will change."

"If pounded into submission?"

Paul's eyes went dark again. Silas cocked his head and looked at him gravely.

"Time is short, Silas, and we should not waste any of it pleasing another person."

"I'll tell Timothy that, the next time he strives to live up to your expectations."

"The Scriptures say a man should remain at home for a year and give his wife pleasure! I say what time we have must be dedicated to spreading the news of Jesus Christ."

"Yes. *You* say."

"We carry the message of life! What is more important than that?"

"Nothing. But it does not have to be carried alone."

"We're not alone. We travel in pairs."

"And some of the pairs could be husband and wife."

Paul's eyes blazed. "The Lord could return tomorrow, Silas. Should we devote ourselves to anything or anyone that does not further the message of Christ?"

"If we don't love others, Paul, what good is all our fine preaching?"

"You're talking about *lust*, not love!"

"Is this discussion about winning a debate, Paul, or about the very real struggles of people within the body of Christ? Some will be called to marry and have children. Will you tell them they are not allowed to do so because *you* are called to celibacy and dedication to evangelism?"

"There is no time for marriage!"

"So, now you know when Jesus will return. Is that what you're saying? Even Jesus said He didn't know! Only the Father knows!"

Silas took a deep breath, realizing his voice had risen in anger. Anger would accomplish nothing. Oh, but Paul could be so adamant, so fiercely stubborn.

"You were called of God to travel and preach, Paul. I've been called, of late, to accompany you. Each of us is called to different tasks and places within society. You have preached so yourself."

"All to build the body—"

"Yes. To build! And if everyone *refuses* to marry or have children, even if God leads them to do so, what happens to our numbers within a generation?"

Paul drew back and frowned.

Silas spread his hands. "God made marriage, Paul. The Lord sanctifies the relationship." He shrugged. "Perhaps the question is not whether men and women should marry, but how they should behave when they do. What is a Christian marriage to look like to the world around us? *Love each other*. What does that mean in terms other than the physical? Peter and his wife have been an inspiration to many. . . ."

Over the months, they had discussed marriage and prayed for God's guidance in what to teach about it. Everywhere they went, they had seen the way unrestrained sexual passion could destroy lives. Such passions were the foundation of idol worship.

Silas took up the reed pen again and ran it between his fingers. When his father died, he'd had no time to consider marriage. The young woman who might have become his wife was given to another with his blessing. The loss had not touched his heart. He had barely known her.

He wanted to know Diana and, because of these feelings, did his best to avoid her.

But she was always at meetings, sitting nearby, attentive. It took determined efforts on his part to keep his gaze from drifting back to her. And her smile . . .

He could not allow himself to think of her. It led him to thoughts of what might have been and could never be.

Mixing another supply of ink, Silas set his own scroll aside and worked until late copying Peter's letters. Only then did he allow himself to linger on his past again.

+   +   +

PAUL *and I planned to go to Asia, but were prevented when Roman foot soldiers stopped us on the road and enlisted us to carry their gear. They demanded only the distance Roman law allowed. We saw this as an opportunity to tell them about Jesus and traveled with them all the way to the border of Mysia. We prayed about whether God wanted us to cross the mountains into Asia, but the Holy Spirit sent us north instead, and then east along the border of Bithynia and on to Troas.*

We knew the Lord had led us there. Troas is a strategic meeting point of sea routes on the northwestern coast of Asia, southwest of the old city of Troy. Its position close to the mouth of the Hellespont has made the Roman colony grow. The citizens have made harbor basins, which provide shelter from the northerlies for ships. Troas is the main port for crossing to Neapolis in Macedonia and reaching the land route to Rome. The Good News could spread easily in all directions from Troas.

We met Luke, the physician, in Troas. Paul needed salve for an infection, and Luke was recommended to us. What a great friend he became, not just to Paul and Timothy and me, but to other brothers and sisters. He left his practice to join us in our travels. As soon as he accepted Christ, the Holy Spirit filled him with purpose, that of gathering facts and information about Jesus' birth, teaching, miracles, death, burial, and resurrection. When he was not attending someone as a physician, he could be found hard at work compiling his reports.

When we were in Ephesus, Luke spoke for long hours with Mary, the mother of Jesus, and John the apostle, with

whom she lived. He met Lazarus and his sisters before they
sailed to Tarsus. In Jerusalem, he spoke to James and several
disciples. If he ever completes this history, the church can
know it is a trustworthy account.

While we were in Troas, Paul had a vision. "A man of
Macedonia keeps calling out to me, 'Come over here and
help us!'"

The four of us sailed to Samothrace and reached Neapolis
the next day. We only stayed long enough to eat and rest
before we headed for Philippi.

We were all excited about what the Lord would do, for
Philippi, a prosperous Roman colony, was on the Egnatian
Way, the military road that joined Rome and the East. It
was along this great highway that information traveled from
one end of the empire to the other. From Troas, the message
would travel by sea; from Philippi, by land.

We spent several days looking for a synagogue.

Paul grew dismayed. "We must be the only Jews in the
entire city." All it required to establish a synagogue was ten
men who were heads of households.

On the Sabbath, we went outside the city in search of
a place of prayer under the open sky and near a river. We
found a suitable place where the road crossed the Gangites
River. Several women were already gathered there, praying.
While Luke, Timothy, and I hesitated, Paul walked down
the bank.

"Come on." He motioned to us to follow.

One of the servant girls looked at Timothy and whispered
to her friend, who giggled.

A woman in a fine tunic with purple trim took charge.
Shushing the girls, she stood and gave Paul an imperious
look. "We are Jews seeking a quiet place to worship God."

I took those words as a plea for us to leave. Paul was not so easily shaken.

"We are Jews also," Paul told her. "And these two are devout men of God." He introduced each of us. "We bring you Good News."

The woman frowned. "What do you mean by 'Good News'?"

"We are followers of the Lord's Messiah, Jesus. He was crucified, buried, and raised from the dead after three days. This man—" he pointed to me—"saw Jesus numerous times and saw Him ascend into heaven."

"Please." She gestured, seating herself on an expensive Babylonian blanket. "Join us." Timothy and Luke held back. "All of you." She smiled. "I am Lydia from Thyatira. I'm a merchant in Philippi. I sell purple fabrics. And these are my servants—good young ladies, all of them." She gave a pointed look at one who had sidled closer to Timothy and patted the place beside her. The girl obeyed. "Tell us more about this Jesus," Lydia said.

We did, with great pleasure. She listened intently and believed every word. So did those with her. "Is there any reason we cannot be baptized here?" Lydia wanted to know. "Today?"

Paul laughed. "None!"

The younger ones laughed joyfully and splashed one another in their exuberance, while Lydia stood on the bank, dripping with dignity. "Please, come to my house. I have plenty of room, and you may stay for as long as you like."

Paul shook his head. "We are thankful for your generous invitation, Lydia, but we wouldn't want to make things difficult for you."

"I have a *large* house, Paul."

"Even in Macedonia, I'm certain neighbors might wonder what four strange men are doing in your house."

She dismissed his argument with a wave of her hand. "If you agree that I am a true believer in the Lord, come and stay at my home. My neighbors know me, and I will make certain they soon know you. You can tell them all you have told me."

Lydia's house was indeed large, and she treated us as honored guests. Within a few days, we had started a small church in her house. We often went back to the river to baptize new believers and preach to those who stopped to watch.

And then the trouble began, as it so often did when many came to Christ.

A slave girl began to follow us from the city one day. She shouted at everyone. "These men are servants of the Most High God, and they have come to tell you how to be saved."

Paul stopped and faced her.

Lydia shook her head. "Leave her alone, Paul. You will only bring trouble on all of us if you argue with her. She's a famous fortune-teller. Her owners are among the leaders of the city, and they make great sums of money off her prophecies."

I glanced back at the girl. "She's speaking the truth right now."

"Not out of love," Paul said.

She went as far as the city gate. Her face looked grotesque, and her body twitched as she pointed at us. "Those men are servants of the Most High God. . . ."

A few who had started to follow us were afraid to pass by her.

The next day, she followed us again. This time she came

out through the city gates, and stood on the road above the riverbank. Paul tried to preach, but she kept shouting. No one could concentrate on anything Paul or Timothy or I said. Everyone kept looking up at that poor, wretched, demon-possessed girl.

When she followed us yet again, we tried to approach and speak with her. She fled into the house of one of her owners. "You have to pay to see her," the guard told Paul.

"I didn't come to hear her prophesy, but to speak with her."

"No one talks to her unless they pay the master first."

We discussed the situation. "All we can do is ignore her," I said, "and hope she will tire of this."

"And in the meantime, our brothers and sisters learn nothing."

"Continue to meet in my house."

"There are already too many, Lydia. Many more can gather at the river."

"If you confront her, you will only bring trouble down on us."

Every day for days on end, the slave girl followed us, shouting. I saw anguish as well as anger in her face and was reminded of Mary Magdalene, from whom Jesus had cast out seven demons that had tormented her. I prayed, but the girl continued to follow.

Though I pitied the girl, Paul grew increasingly frustrated.

"Nothing can be accomplished with all her shouting and screaming. The demon distracts us from teaching and others from hearing the Word of God!"

When she ran up close behind us and screamed in rage, Paul turned on her.

"*Silence, demon!*" He pointed at her. *"I command you in the name of Jesus Christ to come out of her and never enter her again!"*

The girl stood for a moment, eyes wide, and then gave a long sigh. I caught her before she fell. People ran to see what had happened, clustering close.

"Is she dead?"

"He's killed her."

"She's alive," Luke said. "Give her room to breathe!"

She roused, her face smooth in wonder. "It's gone." A child's voice, perplexed, hopeful.

"Yes." I set her upon her feet. "The demon is gone."

Her eyes filled with fear. "It'll come back."

Paul put his hand on her shoulder. "No. If you accept Jesus as Lord, He will fill you with the Holy Spirit, and no demon will ever possess you again."

"Who is Jesus?"

"Let me through!" A man shouted at the back of the crowd. "Get out of my way!" He pushed toward us. One look into her face and he grew alarmed. "What have you done?" He grasped the girl by the arm and held her close at his side. "What did you do to her?"

Everyone spoke at once.

"They cast out a demon!"

"This man told her to be silent."

"He called the demon out of her."

The man thrust the girl toward Paul. "Call it back into her!"

"Jesus . . ." The girl covered her face and sobbed. "Jesus."

"Shut up, girl. Now is not the time." He glared at Paul. "You'd better do what I say."

"Never."

"You've ruined her, and you'll pay for it!"

Others arrived claiming to own her and joined in haranguing Paul.

"You will make her as she was, or we'll sue you."

"Our livelihood depends on her."

Men grabbed hold of us, shouting. Punched and shoved, I lost my footing. Dragged up, I spotted Paul, mouth bleeding. Timothy and Luke shouted in our defense, but were pushed aside. "Get out of here! We have no quarrel with you!"

The girl's owners hauled us none too gently to the marketplace. "These men have destroyed our property!"

The officials tried to calm the men, but they grew more vitriolic. "Call the chief magistrate. He knows of our girl. She's prophesied for him several times, to his benefit. Tell him she can no longer prophesy because of what these Jews have done! He'll judge in our favor!"

When the chief magistrate came out, the men shouted even louder against us, adding false accusations. "The whole city is in an uproar because of these Jews! You know what trouble they are, and here they come to our city now teaching customs that are illegal for us Romans to practice!"

"That's not true!" Paul called out.

I fought the hands that held me. "Allow us to declare our case!" A man struck me in the side of the head.

The man who had come for the girl shouted, "It is forbidden, for Romans are not allowed to engage in any religion not sanctioned by the emperor!"

"Emperor Claudius has expelled all Jews from Rome because of the trouble they cause. . . ."

"They speak against our gods!"

Their hatred of us grew to encompass all Jews.

Paul shouted. "We speak only of the Lord Jesus Christ, Savior—"

"They are causing chaos!"

The chief magistrates ordered us beaten.

I called out. "The Lord has sent us to tell you the Good News. . . ."

None listened.

"Show them what happens to Jews who cause trouble!"

Hands dug into me. Pulled, yanked, shoved, my robe torn from my back, I found myself stretched out and tied to a post. The first lash of the rod sent a shock of pain through my body, and I cried out.

I could hear Paul. "The Lord has sent us to tell you the Good News. Jesus is Lord! He offers salvation. . . ." Blows rained upon him.

The second and third blows drove the breath from my body. I clawed at the post, twisting against the ropes that held me, but there was no escaping the pain. Paul and I hung side by side, bodies jerking with each blow. I opened my mouth wide to gasp for breath and thought of Jesus hanging on the cross. "Father, forgive them," Jesus had said. "They don't know what they are doing."

I closed my eyes tightly, gritted my teeth, and prayed for the flogging to end.

I don't know how many blows we took before the magistrate ordered us cut down and thrown into prison. Paul was unconscious. I feared they had killed him. I longed for death. Every movement sent spears of agony.

They dragged us to the jailer. "Guard them securely! If they escape, your life is forfeit!"

He ordered us carried down to the inner dungeon. They

dumped us on cold stone inside a cell and fastened our feet in stocks. I gagged at the foul smell of human excrement, urine, fear-inspired sweat, and death. I tried to rise, but collapsed again. My back throbbed and burned. Weak, I couldn't move, and I lay in a pool of my own blood.

Paul lay close by, unmoving. "Paul!" He stirred. Weeping, I thanked God. I reached out and gripped his wrist gently. "It's over."

Moaning, he rolled his head toward me. "I had you beaten once. This may be a hint of atonement."

"Perhaps, if I hadn't received the same treatment." I gave him a pained grin. "And as I remember, you kicked me three times. No one used a wooden rod on me."

"I won't argue with you."

I gave a soft laugh and winced. "My consolation."

Gritting my teeth, I sucked in my breath and managed to sit up. Chains jingled as Paul slowly did the same. We leaned forward, resting our arms on our raised knees, waiting until the pain in our backs subsided enough so that we could breathe normally.

"By God's grace, we share in Christ's suffering." Paul raised his head. "We have company."

Looking out through the bars of our cell, I saw other men in the dungeon with us—silent, dark-eyed men without hope, waiting for an end to their ordeal.

Paul smiled at me. "Even in a dungeon, God gives us opportunities."

And so he preached. "By God's great mercy, He washed away our sins, giving us a new birth and new life through the Holy Spirit, which He generously poured out upon us through Christ Jesus, our Savior."

I considered it a privilege to suffer for the name of Jesus

Christ, to share in some way the sufferings my Lord endured for me. I counted it an honor to suffer with Paul.

We sang songs of deliverance in that dark place, and laughed we did, for the sound filled that great, yawning hole where human misery dwelt. We rejoiced in our salvation, our rescue from sin and death, our assurance in the promises of God and heaven. Our voices rose and swelled, flowing along stone corridors to the guards. They did not order us to be silent. We had a congregation in that prison. Chained, yes, but undistracted by a girl's raving. Rapt and eager, they listened to the only hope in a living hell on earth.

One confessed to committing murder. Paul said he had also, and told how God had forgiven, reclaimed, and set him on a new path.

Another declared his innocence. Once I had thought myself innocent and above reproach. I told him all men are sinners in need of grace.

An earthquake came around midnight and shook the foundations of the prison house. Stone grated against stone, and dust billowed around us. Men screamed in fear. The prison doors burst open. The chains around our ankles fell off as though unlocked by invisible hands.

"What's happening?" Men cried out, confused, afraid to hope.

"It is the Lord's doing!" Paul answered. "Stay as you are. Only trust in Him!"

Running steps approached, and I caught sight of the jailer. He looked around frantically, saw opened cells in horror, and drew his sword. When he removed his breastplate, we knew what he meant to do. Death by his own sword would be preferable to crucifixion for dereliction of duty. He thought we had all escaped!

"Stop!" Paul shouted. "Don't kill yourself! Do no harm to yourself! No one has left! We are all here!"

Lowering his sword, the jailer shouted for torches. Guards ran toward our cell, filling it with torchlight. The jailer fell on his knees before us.

"Get up!" Paul told him. "We're not gods that you should worship us. We came with a message of salvation."

A prisoner called out. "They speak of a god who died and rose again."

"And still lives," another joined in.

"Come out of here!" The jailer beckoned, shaking, his eyes wide with fear. "Come out!"

He led us out of the prison and took us to his house in the compound. He called for water, salve, and bandages. A woman hovered, several children clutching at her. She kept her arm around them as she spoke to the jailer. "I feared for you, my husband. The gods are angry. They shook the foundations of our house!"

"It's all right now, Lavinia. Hush! These men serve a god of great power."

"He is the only God!" Paul said. "There is no other."

The jailer stared at us. "Sirs, what must I do to be saved?"

"Believe in the Lord Jesus Christ," Paul told him, "and you will be saved."

I smiled at the woman and children. "Along with everyone in your household."

"The earthquake that brought your freedom is proof of His great power." The jailer took the basin of water from a servant and washed our wounds himself. "Tell me about this God who can open prison doors and remove chains."

The jailer—whose name, we learned, was Demetrius—and

his family believed everything we told them. We baptized them. Not even a dungeon could shut out the light of Jesus Christ!

Food was prepared, and we broke bread together.

"How can I return you to the prison when you've brought us life? I will send word to your friends. I'll get you out of the city. They can meet you with supplies. . . ."

For a moment, I was tempted. Thankfully, Paul declined. "We will not flee. We obey the law. God can rescue us from the false accusations that put us in prison."

Guards took us back to our cell.

A few hours later, Demetrius returned. "I sent word to the magistrates and told them what happened last night, of the earthquake. They felt it, too. When I told them about the cell doors opening and your shackles falling away, they said to let you go. You are free to leave Philippi."

"Free to leave?" I said. "Or ordered to leave?"

"They want you out of the city."

Disappointment filled me. We had accomplished so much. But there was still so much to do. The Lord had saved this man and his household, and now, unknown to him, Satan was using him to silence us.

Paul put his hands on his knees. "We're not leaving!"

"You have no choice!" Guards waited outside to escort us out of the city.

"They have publicly beaten us without a trial and put us in prison—and we are Roman citizens. So now they want us to leave secretly? Certainly not! Let them come themselves to release us!"

Demetrius blanched. "You're Romans? You should have said something!"

I smiled wryly. "They never gave us the chance."

Demetrius sent the message. He returned with the officials. The man who had ordered us flogged stood pale-faced with fear of retribution. "I beg your forgiveness. Had we known you were Roman citizens, we would never have allowed anyone to lay hands on you let alone seen you beaten in the marketplace!"

"Please believe us!"

"You judged us without trial, based on false accusations," Paul said. "And now you banish us from Philippi."

"No, no, you misunderstand us!" The chief magistrate spread his hands. "Crispus, Pontus, and the others swayed me with their accusations. They are still furious over their slave girl. And they have cause. The girl is worthless now."

What would happen to the poor girl? I wondered. "If she's worthless, tell her owners to sell her to Lydia, the merchant who sells purple cloth." She would free the girl.

"There will be trouble if you remain in Philippi," said another.

They insisted. "We cannot promise your safety if you remain here."

"We accept your apology," Paul told them.

"And you will leave." Clearly, they wanted us gone as soon as possible.

Paul nodded. I wanted to argue, but he gave a look that silenced me. "As soon as we meet with others of our faith."

We went to Lydia's house, where we found Luke and Timothy. They had been praying all night. "God has answered your prayers," I said, laughing despite the discomfort of my wounds.

Luke checked the dressing. "More needs to be done." When he added salt to prevent infection, I passed out.

Paul roused before I did and asked that the believers

gather. When they all arrived, we gave them what instructions we could in the little time we had. "Be strong in the Lord and in His mighty power," Paul said.

I promised we would write to them.

Paul and I, with Luke and Timothy, left Philippi late that afternoon.

Of all the churches I helped plant over the years, the Philippian believers suffered the greatest hardships. Some lost their lives; many, their homes and businesses. Yet, they remained steadfast. Though impoverished by persecution, God made them rich in faith and love.

May the grace of our Lord Jesus Christ continue to sustain them until the day Jesus returns.

FIVE

WE TRAVELED *through Amphipolis and Apollonia and on to Thessalonica. We found a synagogue and stayed with Jason, a Jew who had accepted Christ in Jerusalem years before during Pentecost. We did not want to be a burden to him. Paul found work as a tentmaker; I wrote letters and documents. Every Sabbath, we went to the synagogue and reasoned with the Jews. We showed them proofs through the Scriptures that Jesus is the Messiah of God, the Christ whom God sent to fulfill the Law and ransom us from sin and death, but few believed.*

The greatest number of new believers came from among the God-fearing Greeks who followed the teachings of the Torah. They embraced Christ with zeal and spread word through the city about Jesus. Many Jews became incensed as the number of believers grew. Finding troublemakers in the agora, they formed a mob and descended upon Jason's house, expecting to find Paul and me there. Paul worked just outside the city, and I was off somewhere helping an official write a letter. So they grabbed Jason along with a few others and dragged these poor men before the city authorities.

It happened just as it had in Philippi!

They accused Jason and the other believers they'd seized of causing chaos, when it was they who stirred the city into confusion. They claimed we taught Jesus was a king like Caesar and that we encouraged the people to rebel against Rome!

I found friends of my father and arranged for bond to be paid. Jason and the others were set free. But the trouble was far from over.

Jason insisted Paul and I leave the city. "The Jews are

intent upon killing Paul. They despise you, too, Silas, but see you as a Greek. They see Paul as a traitor to his race and a priest of apostasy. Every word he speaks is blasphemy to their ears, and they will stop at nothing to kill him if he remains here. You must go. *Now!*"

"I'll go with you," Timothy said, packed and ready.

"You will stay here with Luke." Paul remained adamant despite Timothy's plea. "We will meet later." I knew Paul feared for the boy and did not want to put him in danger, and he entrusted him to Luke.

We left under cover of darkness and headed for Berea. We went straight to the synagogue there. I expected more trouble, but we found the Berean Jews open-minded and open of heart. They listened and then examined the Scriptures to see if what we said was true. The body of Christ grew rapidly in Berea as Jews and prominent Greeks, both men and women, embraced Christ.

Luke and Timothy arrived, eager to help. On their heels came some of the Thessalonican Jewish leaders, who had taken such offense to our teaching. They intended to destroy the church. "You must head south," the Berean believers told us.

Paul did not want to leave. "We cannot abandon these lambs, Silas."

I feared for his life. Luke and Timothy joined in my efforts to persuade him, but Paul protested. "It is stubbornness and pride that brings these Thessalonicans after me again. I will not give in to them."

"Is that not pride speaking, Paul?" Harsh words, I knew, but sometimes that was the only way to get through to Paul. "Do not give sin an opportunity. If we leave, they will disperse, thinking this flock cannot survive without a shepherd."

"Will they?"

"The seed has taken root in them, Paul. They know the truth and the truth has set them free. The Holy Spirit and the Scriptures will guide them. We must go for their sake as well as yours."

The more difficult parting took place at the coast. We had only enough money for two passages to Athens. "You've been ill. Luke must go with you."

"You know the respect and love I have for Luke, Silas, but I chose *you*."

"The wound on your back continues to fester. You need a physician more than a coworker."

"I'll be fine!"

"Yes, you will, with the proper care God wants you to have."

"But—"

I lost patience. "Don't argue! Why must you always argue, even with those who believe as you do! Now, bridle your tongue, and get on that boat!"

He laughed. I was immediately ashamed at my loss of temper. "There are other lost sheep, Paul. Think of them. And don't forget God called you to be His chosen instrument to bear His name before the Gentiles and kings and people of Israel. You cannot remain here and let them kill you. Kings, Paul! That's what the Lord told Ananias! Perhaps one day you'll speak before Caesar, and God willing, the emperor will listen. You must go now. God wants it so!"

He wept.

I embraced him. "You are by far the more persuasive preacher among us." I did not speak from flattery. When I drew back, I gripped his arms. "Your life must not end here."

"What of you and Timothy?"

"We'll go back to Berea and live quietly. We will teach and encourage our brothers and sisters and join you later."

Paul embraced Timothy. The boy wept.

"Come, Paul!" Luke said. "We must go!"

I held firm to Timothy's shoulder as the two men boarded the ship. "God will watch over him, Timothy. We'll stay until they leave the harbor. Just in case our good friend decides to jump ship."

Timothy gave a broken laugh. "He might. He worries about me."

"You must learn to stand without him, Timothy. He is called to spread the Good News. Others are called to remain behind and teach."

He looked up at me. "Not yet."

"Soon." God had told me so.

Life would never be easy for Paul.

Nor for anyone who traveled with him.

+ + +

While we waited for word from Paul and Luke, Timothy and I found work to support ourselves and met with believers each evening. I taught; Timothy encouraged.

We received frequent letters from Paul and Luke about their progress in Athens. Our friend had not gone into hiding.

"I spoke in the synagogues, but the Athenian Jews have hearts of stone. I now preach in the public square, where people are more willing to listen."

But Athens grieved his spirit.

"I cannot turn right or left without coming face-to-face with an idol that promotes debauchery and licentious behavior. The people flock to these gods."

He met a few Epicurean and Stoic philosophers in the marketplace.

"Athenians crave new ideas, and the message of Christ intrigues them. They invited me to speak on the Areopagus before the council. I went, praying the Lord would give me the words to reach the hearts of these people. God answered my prayer when I saw an altar with the inscription, 'To an Unknown God.' Jesus is the Unknown God. All but a few thought me a babbler proclaiming a strange deity. They laughed when I told them of Jesus' resurrection. Yet, a few are saved. You will meet Dionysius when you come. He is a member of the council. Another believer is Damaris, a woman of good reputation. We hold meetings in Dionysius's house daily. He lives near the Areopagus."

The next letter came from Luke.

"We have moved south to Corinth."

He did not say why, but I imagine Paul was driven out of town again, either by the Jews or members of the council.

"We met two Jews expelled from Italy by Emperor Claudius's edict. Priscilla and Aquila are tentmakers and have invited Paul to join in their business. I am staying with them as well. Paul is exhausted, but I cannot stop him from working. When he isn't sewing hides together, he is in the synagogue debating with the Jews and Greeks. He needs help. I am a doctor, not an orator. Come as soon as you can. We have great need of both you and Timothy."

I had earned barely enough for my passage, but when the Bereans heard of Paul's need, they raised funds to pay for Timothy's passage. Timothy wrote a beautiful statement of faith to encourage them. "If we die with Him, we will also live with Him. If we endure hardship, we will reign with Him. If we deny Him, He will deny us. If we are unfaithful,

He remains faithful, for He cannot deny who He is." I made a copy to give to Paul.

Later, Paul used these same words to encourage Timothy when he was shepherd to the flock in Ephesus, a place of such evil practices we all thought it the throne of Satan himself.

Timothy's words encourage me now.

We all must face persecution because of the evil that grips this world. Yet, Jesus Christ is Lord! I know this: our future is secure! I know this, too: Christ reigns in our hearts, minds, souls. Our lives are living testimonies of the truth of Jesus Christ, crucified, buried, and raised.

One day, Jesus will return, and the days of tribulation will be over.

Come, Lord Jesus. Come soon.

——————————————— ✢   ✢   ✢ ———————————————

"CAN you not rest awhile, Silas?"

His heart leaped at the sound of Diana's voice. He turned and saw her in the doorway. "What are you doing here?"

"Epanetus sent me." She looked embarrassed. "I don't know why he thought I might be able to get you to leave this room."

"Is Curiatus with you?"

"He's in the garden."

Silas put the reed pen in its case and rose.

"Are you in pain?" She came a step closer.

He held up his hand. "No. I get stiff from sitting so long."

"Sitting too long isn't good for anyone, Silas."

The caring in her voice made his heart drum. He sought a way to build walls. "I'm old."

"You are no older than my husband would have been had he lived."

He looked at her then. There had been no wistfulness in her voice, no sorrow. "How long ago did he die?"

"Five years."

They looked at each other for a long moment, silent. She gave a soft gasp. He felt the heat climb into his face. "I'm sorry," he said roughly.

She held his gaze.

He swallowed hard and avoided her gaze. "We should join the others."

———————————— ✦ ✦ ✦ ————————————

IT WAS *an easy voyage to Athens, though I, not being much of a sailor, spent most of it with my head over the gunwales.*

We met Priscilla and Aquila and liked them immediately. They had accepted Christ within hours of meeting Paul in the synagogue. "Paul is very persuasive." They proved good friends to their mentor.

Luke returned to writing his history and giving care to those in need, especially Paul, who suffered chronic pain. The beatings had taken a toll on his body, and his vision was impaired. He could no longer write, except in large letters. "I need a secretary now more than ever," he told me. I was honored to serve in that capacity.

Timothy quickly found work in Corinth, as did I. We made enough to support ourselves and Paul. This proved a great blessing, for Paul was able to dedicate himself to preaching. We assisted him by instructing those who accepted Christ.

Letters arrived from Thessalonica, filled with attacks against Paul's integrity and the message we preached. Several beloved brothers had been killed for their faith in Christ, and their friends and relatives now questioned Paul's teachings. They had expected the Lord to come before anyone died. A few took advantage of the confusion, and proclaimed Paul a liar who preached only for profit.

I had never seen Paul so hurt by accusations. How he grieved! I was more angry than Paul. Who taught with more risk to their lives than Paul? No one!

Tears streamed down his cheeks. "Such is the work of Satan!"

I felt defeated. All our work! All our prayers! The converts forgot all the sound teaching and listened to lies!

"We must go back and confront these false teachers before they turn our brothers and sisters away from Christ!"

I felt like flotsam, moving back and forth on the tide. If Paul wanted to go, I would go. If Paul wanted to stay, I would stay. I had come on this journey to stand beside him no matter the risk. If left to myself, I might have gotten on the first ship sailing for Caesarea!

We made it as far as Athens and had to wait. Paul fell ill again. I cared for him as best I could, but he needed a doctor. "I'm sending for Luke."

"No!" Paul lay pale, but vehement as ever in his opinions. "I will be all right in a few days. Luke is needed where he is. God can heal me, if He wills. And if not, then this is a burden I must carry."

As soon as Paul was well enough, we set out again, only to be attacked near the port and stripped of our passage money. Damaris helped us, but one thing after another happened to keep us from going north. "Perhaps it is the Lord keeping us here, Paul," I pointed out.

Paul, still not fully well, grew impatient. "It is Satan who delays us! We can't wait any longer! Someone must go to Thessalonica and tell our brothers and sisters the truth before their faith is murdered by lies."

Timothy said he would go. We laid hands on him, blessed him, and sent him off, eager to defend Paul and explain more fully Jesus' promise to return. I admit I feared the young man's natural reserve might keep him from being effective. Paul worried he might be killed. We both prayed unceasingly.

It was not an easy time for us.

Paul's health grew worse, and he fell into a deep depression. "I'm afraid all we've worked so hard to accomplish is lost."

We could do nothing but pray and trust in the Lord. The waiting proved a greater test of our faith than floggings and imprisonment!

But God was faithful!

Timothy returned zealous and with good reports. Rejoicing, we three returned to Corinth, renewed in faith and strength. Our good spirits dampened again though when, after a few weeks, the Corinthian Jews refused to believe a word Paul or I said. No matter how much proof we showed from the Scriptures, they hardened their hearts against Jesus. The last time Paul entered the synagogue, the gathering storm burst forth and some who despised Paul insulted and blasphemed Jesus to his face.

"Your blood is upon your own heads!" Paul cried out and left the synagogue. He stood outside, shaking his robes in protest. "I shake the dust of this place from me!" He raised his arm. "You and you and you." He pointed to specific men. "I am innocent. Let your blood be on your own heads, for you have rejected the Lord God. From now on, I will go preach to the Gentiles!"

The neighborhood remained in an uproar that day and for days following.

Paul might say he consigned them to God's wrath, but in truth the man refused to give up hope. I laugh now, for he moved in with Titius Justus, a Gentile believer. Titius lived right next door to the synagogue!

Not a day went by that the Jews did not see Paul receiving visitors. Crispus, one of their leaders, came to reason with Paul. Away from the sway and jealousy of the others, he received Christ. Soon, Crispus brought his entire family to hear about Jesus. Our enemies ground their teeth and muttered at those who came. Jews and Gentiles under one roof, breaking bread together? The Christ of God for all men? The hard-hearted refused to believe.

Paul received constant threats, and, as his friends, so did Timothy and I and others. But the attacks were far worse upon him. He became afraid. I am convinced that his fear rose from exhaustion. He worked constantly, from before dawn to long after dark. Even a man of his amazing stamina needs to rest. I certainly did. But Paul felt compelled to preach, compelled to answer every question with proof, compelled to pour himself out like a liquid offering. When he was not preaching, he studied the scrolls we carried, preparing for the next battle. He dictated letters far into the night.

A tired man is more easily shaken.

"I'm afraid," he confessed to me one night. "It's one thing for people to attack me, but my friends . . ." His eyes filled with tears. "I'm afraid of what my enemies will do next, Silas, who they might harm because of what I say." I knew he feared for Timothy, and not without cause. But Timothy was as on fire for Christ as he. The young man had given his life as a living sacrifice for the Lord.

"You must do whatever the Lord tells you to do, Paul. If the Lord says speak, you already know you have Timothy's blessing. And mine as well."

Titius Justus wondered if Paul should press on. "He has good reason to be afraid, Silas." Titius told me Paul received threats every time he left the house. The day before, the Judaizers had cornered Paul in the marketplace, and said they would kill him if he continued. When I confronted Paul about this, he said it was true.

"Perhaps we should move on again. We have planted the seeds. God will water and make them grow."

Paul smiled bleakly. "It will be the same anywhere I go, Silas. You know that as well as I."

Trouble followed Paul in the same way trouble had followed Jesus.

How many times had I seen the Good News greeted with anger and scorn? Most people don't want to hear the truth, let alone embrace it. To accept Christ's gift means admitting that everything on which we based our lives before has gained us nothing. It means surrendering to a power greater than ourselves. Few want to surrender to anything but their lusts. We cling to our vanity and go on striving to find our own way when there is only one way.

I praised God every time I saw truth dawn in someone's eyes, the veil of Satan's lies dissolved, a heart of stone beating with new life. The new believer stood on a mountaintop looking out at the vast hope laid wide open before them, an eternal, lifelong journey with the Lord. They became a living, breathing temple in which God dwelled. The rebirth was a miracle as great as Jesus' feeding thousands on a few loaves of bread and fish, because it was evidence He lived; His promises continued to be fulfilled daily.

But fear sets in so easily.

We decided to be cautious. We thought it wise, but, in truth, Paul was silenced, and so was I. We had forgotten we must step out in faith, not sit and wait for it to grow in shadows.

By the grace of God, Jesus spoke to Paul in a vision. "Don't be afraid! Speak out!" Jesus said many people in the city already belonged to Him. All we had to do was go out and find them!

We obeyed. With such great encouragement, how could we not?

We set out, faith renewed, zeal restored.

For eighteen months.

And then a new governor came to Achaia, and everything changed again.

Soon after Gallio took office, the Jews rose up against Paul, took him to the judgment seat and accused him of teaching men to worship God in ways contrary to Roman law. But Gallio was not like Pontius Pilate, easily swayed by a mob. Paul did not even say a word in his own defense before Gallio ended the session.

"Since this is merely a question of words and names and your Jewish law, take care of it yourselves. I refuse to judge such matters." With a jerk of his head, guards moved and drove the Jews away from the judgment seat.

Greeks grabbed hold of Sosthenes, the leader of the synagogue, and began beating him. Gallio continued to conduct business and ignore the fracas. A Gentile punched Sosthenes, knocked him down, and kicked him right there before the judgment seat.

Paul tried to push through. "Stop!" Unwittingly, he used Aramaic.

I cried out in Greek and then Latin. They withdrew, leaving Sosthenes half conscious and bleeding on the stone pavement. The rabbi's friends were nowhere to be seen. He shrank back from us in fear, though we only wanted to help him.

"Let us help you!"

"Why do you do this for me?" Sosthenes rasped. "You, of all people . . ."

"Because Jesus would do it," Paul said, straining to help lift him.

Sosthenes stumbled, but we kept him from falling. He wept all the way to Priscilla and Aquila's. Luke dressed his wounds. We sent word to the synagogue, but none came for him. They would not enter the house of a Gentile.

When Sosthenes became feverish, we took turns caring for him. We told him about Jesus. "He made the blind see, and the deaf hear. He raised a widow's son and called a friend from the tomb in which he had lain for four days."

I told him of Jesus' trial before Pontius Pilate, of how He died on the cross on Passover, and three days later, arose. I told him of my life in Jerusalem and Caesarea and how it changed on the road to Emmaus. Paul told him of seeing Jesus on the road to Damascus.

Sosthenes tried not to listen at first. He wept and covered his ears. But gradually he did listen. "It was not your words that convinced me," he told us. "It was your love. I was your enemy, Paul, and you and Silas lifted me up."

We baptized him.

He returned to the synagogue, determined to sway the others. He could not.

"It is not by your word or mine that men are saved," Paul told him when he came to Titius's home, "but by the power of the Holy Spirit."

"They are my friends," Sosthenes wept. "My family."

"Continue to love them. And keep praying."

+   +   +

A few months later, Paul decided to go to Cenchrea and fulfill a vow of thanksgiving to the Lord. "Jesus has protected me here in Corinth." The vow required he cut off his hair and shave.

I helped him prepare. "How long will you remain in solitude?"

"Thirty days."

"Will you return here, or do you want us to join you there?"

"You and Timothy must remain here. There is still much work to do. When the time of the vow is complete, Aquila and Priscilla will join me, and we'll sail to Syria."

I was stunned. And hurt. "Are you telling me you no longer need my services?"

He grimaced as though in pain. "Don't look at me like that, Silas. I must go where the Lord leads, even if it means I must leave beloved friends behind."

Paul left the next day. The parting was especially difficult for Timothy, whom Paul commanded to remain with me in Corinth.

The church met in Chloe's home. And what a church it was, made up of reformed thieves, drunkards, idol worshippers, and adulterers. They flocked to Christ, who cleansed them of sin and made them like newborn babies. They rejected their previous practices of promiscuity, homosexuality, and debauchery and dedicated themselves to Christ, living holy lives pleasing to God. They became miracles, living testimony to the power of God to change men and women from the inside out.

Apollos, a Jew from Alexandria, arrived with a letter from Priscilla and Aquila. They commended him to us and asked that we welcome him. We did so, and he proved to be as great an orator as Paul, refuting the Jews with Scripture.

The church of Corinth was firmly established and continued to grow.

When Paul wrote that he intended to visit the churches we had planted in Phrygia and Galatia, I thought it time to rejoin him. Stephanas, Fortunatus, and Achaicus proved themselves as able leaders, along with Sosthenes. We sent word of our plans, but when we reached Ephesus, it was Aquila and Priscilla, and not Paul, who greeted us. "He's gone on to Jerusalem for Passover."

The news alarmed me.

"I should've come sooner and dissuaded him! The high council will look for any opportunity to kill him!"

Timothy was grievously disappointed. "Why didn't he wait?"

"We all tried to dissuade him, Silas, but you know how Paul is when he's determined to do something. There's no stopping him."

When they told me Paul had left his books and papers behind, I knew my friend was well aware of what awaited him in Jerusalem. "Paul would rather run toward death than leave the Jews in darkness."

I thought of going after him, but after much prayer, knew God wanted me in Ephesus.

Timothy was not yet ready to stand alone.

+   +   +

"Landing place" is an apt name for Ephesus. It is the intersection of the coastal road running north to Troas and the western route to Colosse, Laodicea, and beyond. Ships from all over the Roman Empire sailed in and out of its port. With its magnificent road lined with marble columns, its theater, baths, library, agora, and paved streets, Ephesus rivals the grandeur of Rome and its infamous debauchery. The city is temple-warden to the three emperors, each honored by an enormous temple. However, it is the Temple of Artemis that dominates. Four times larger than the Parthenon in Athens, it draws thousands of devotees each year, eager to partake of the most depraved worship man creates. Add to this ships that arrive daily, unloading cages of wild animals from Africa and gladiators for the games.

Ephesus was a great trial to me. Everywhere I looked I saw astounding beauty and knew it housed horrendous sin. I longed for the religiosity of Jerusalem, the struggle of men to follow moral laws, the solitude of scholarly pursuits.

Priscilla and Aquila, already established as tentmakers, gathered believers in their home. They nurtured and taught new believers. Timothy and I preached in the agora. When Apollos returned, he preached with the logic of a Roman and the poetry of a Greek. Crowds gathered to hear him speak, and many came to faith in the Lord through his teaching.

Timothy grew as a teacher. Some questioned him because of his youth, but he was mature in the Lord and ready for leadership. Gaius was a great help to him. Erastus, also, proved helpful. He had been an *aedile* in Corinth, and used his administrative gifts to help the church in Corinth. No one lacked provisions.

We were a motley group, much like our sisters and brothers in Corinth. Repentant idolators, fornicators, adulterers, homosexuals, swindlers, and drunkards—all now living lives above reproach, helping one another and others. I quickly saw more miracles in Ephesus than I had in Israel during those three years that Jesus ministered. The Lord was alive, and His Spirit moved mightily in the midst of beautiful, wretched Ephesus.

When I received a letter from the council asking me to return to Jerusalem, I knew it was time for me to step down and place Timothy in leadership.

Though confident in the Lord, Timothy had little confidence in himself. "I am not ready, Silas."

But the Ephesians were not easily led, and there were always wolves intent upon attacking the flock. "You are ready, Timothy. You have the heart and the knowledge. We are each called to a different task. I must go. You must stay."

"But am I capable?"

I gave him what advice I could. "God has equipped you for the work. Remember: we can ask God for wisdom, and He will give it without rebuking us for the asking. But be sure when you ask Him that your faith is in the Lord alone. Don't waver, Timothy. And don't try to work things out on your own. Trust Jesus to show you the right path. Then take it! When He gives you the words to speak, speak them. Do those things and God will do His work here in Ephesus."

He had good friends to stand with him—Aquila and Priscilla, Apollos, Gaius—all devoted servants of the Lord. I left with saddened heart, but fully confident that the Lord would use Timothy mightily to strengthen the Ephesian church.

It has been years now since I have seen Timothy, though we have exchanged letters. His heart is no less humble,

though the Lord has strengthened him over the years, and
sent others to encourage him, including John, the apostle,
and with him, Jesus' mother, Mary.

Mary has gone to be with the Lord now, but John remains.

+   +   +

Time has a way of turning in upon itself as you grow older.
I cannot remember when some things happened, or how, or
in what sequence events occurred.

Paul's time to depart this world had not yet come. After
a brief stay in Jerusalem, he returned to Antioch, where he
reported on his journey. Then he returned to Ephesus. I was
gone by then, home in Jerusalem. But when I heard, I knew
Timothy would be much relieved to have his mentor back at
his side, and would be all the more strengthened by Paul's
instruction and example.

Luke remained Paul's companion and wrote to me often.
God gave Paul miraculous power, which turned many from
worshipping false gods. Those who made idols caused a riot.
Fearing Paul would be murdered, the church sent him to
Philippi. Timothy went with him, but returned soon after.

Others traveled with Paul after that. Some fell away in
exhaustion. Others could not get along with him. Paul kept
going. He was the most dedicated man I knew. He told
me once, "Faith is a race, and we must run it with all our
strength." I imagine him now wearing the laurel wreath.

I miss him.

Had I remained with him, my suffering might be over
now. But the path the Lord has laid out before me is longer
and winds more than I ever imagined it would.

I, like so many others, thought Jesus would return in a
few days or weeks. Then we thought our Lord would return

in a few months, then a few years. He said He would wait until all the world had the opportunity to hear of Him. And the world is larger than we ever imagined.

Paul planned to go to Gaul and never made it.

But again I digress. A tired man's musings. I waste this scroll.

———————————— + + + ————————————

SILAS wanted to quit the task Epanetus had given him. His neck, back, and shoulders ached. His fingers felt stiff. But it wasn't the physical pain of so many hours laboring at the table. It was remembering the years and miles, the friends saved and lost.

Macombo brought a tray. "Have you finished?"

"No."

"You have lived a rich life."

Silas covered his face with his hands.

That night, he slept deeply and dreamed of Jesus. The Lord filled His nail-scarred hands with grain and cast it in all directions. Seeds took root—tiny shoots rising in deserts, on mountaintops, in small villages and great cities. Some drifted on the sea toward distant lands.

Jesus placed a scroll in Silas's hand and smiled.

———————————— + + + ————————————

PAUL *felt drawn back to Jerusalem. Like me, it was his home, the center of all we had known and held dear. The Temple was still the house of God. I could not go up the steps and stand in the corridors and not think of Jesus or hear His voice echoing in my mind. My heart ached every time I stepped foot in that place meant to be holy and now so defiled by corruption.*

We received word Paul had arrived in Caesarea. He stayed

with Philip the Evangelist and his four daughters, all unmarried and with the gift of prophecy. They, like others—myself
included—had chosen not to marry, but to await the return
of the Lord. Agabus went to see Paul. He'd had a dream that
Paul would be imprisoned if he came to Jerusalem.

Paul refused to go into hiding.

When Paul and Luke reached Jerusalem, Mnason welcomed them to his home. I would have enjoyed offering
them hospitality, but my circumstances had changed over
the years, and I no longer owned a house in Jerusalem or
Caesarea. I did not see Paul or Luke until they came to the
council, but when I did, it was clear nothing had changed
between us.

"Silas!" Paul embraced me. I wept with joy. I had such
mixed feelings about him being in Jerusalem. While I longed
for our deep conversations, I feared he would be hunted
down and killed. The Pharisees had never forgiven him for
abandoning their cause. James and all the council members
greeted him warmly. We all shared the same concerns about
his welfare.

Paul gave a good account of his journeys, often calling
upon me to add anything he might have forgotten regarding the cities we had visited together. He had forgotten
little.

Of course, Paul longed to go to the Temple. James and I
had discussed this possibility with the others and thought
trouble might be averted if Paul took with him four men who
had completed vows. By joining them in the purification
ceremony and paying for their hair to be shaved, perhaps the
Jews would see he had not rejected the Law.

Men plan, but God prevails.

Paul went to the Temple. He spent seven days worshipping there, rejoicing in the Lord. And then some Jews from Asia saw him, and spoke out against him. "Everywhere this man goes, he brings trouble upon us!"

I sought to defend him. "You bring trouble upon yourself by rousing mobs and causing riots!"

When anger meets anger, nothing good comes of it.

Accusations filled the air. Some claimed Paul had brought Greeks into the Temple to defile the holy place. Trophimus the Ephesian had been seen near the Temple, and they assumed Paul had brought him inside. The Jewish leaders grabbed Paul and dragged him from the Temple. They threw him outside and slammed the doors. Others began beating him. I cried out for them to stop and found myself in the midst of the fray.

Never had the sight of Roman soldiers and centurions so pleased me as that day! We would have died without their intervention. They surrounded Paul, and used their shields to keep the Jews back. The commander drew his sword and pounded it on his shield. "Quiet! All of you!" He shouted in heavily accented Aramaic, and then commanded his soldiers in Greek. "Put that man in chains until I find out what's going on this time!"

Paul swayed under the weight of iron while the commander tried to gather the facts. "Who is this man you're trying to kill? What has he done?"

"He stirs up dissension!"

"He's desecrated the Temple of our God!"

"He's Saul of Tarsus, and unjustly accused. . . ." We tried to come to his defense. Someone punched me in the side of the head. By the grace of God, I overcame the temptation to swing back.

"He's the ringleader of a cult that defies Rome!"

Everyone shouted, each with a different answer, none near the truth.

Two soldiers hauled Paul up the steps of the barracks while others faced the crowd, shields locked in a wall of protection. Somehow Paul convinced the commander to let him speak to the crowd.

When Paul called out in Hebrew, the Jews fell silent. "I am a Jew, born in Tarsus, a city in Cilicia, and I was brought up and educated here in Jerusalem under Gamaliel. As his student, I was carefully trained in our Jewish laws and customs. I became very zealous to honor God in everything I did, just like all of you today. And I persecuted the followers of the Way." He confessed the bloodguilt of holding the coats while others stoned Stephen, and going after others in his zeal against Christians, even traveling to Damascus to transport Christians from there to Jerusalem for punishment.

"As I was on the road, approaching Damascus about noon, a very bright light from heaven suddenly shone down around me. I fell to the ground and heard a voice saying to me, 'Saul, Saul, why are you persecuting me?'"

They listened intently until he told them how God called on him to take the message of Christ to the Gentiles. Wrath came upon them like a fire.

Men ripped off their cloaks in protest and threw dust into the air.

"Away with such a fellow!"

"Kill him!"

"He isn't fit to live!"

Friends grabbed me and pulled me against a wall and we watched the mob surge up the steps, trying to reach Paul. The commander shouted. Soldiers locked shields. Men fell back, tumbling into others. Some fell, trampled by those still pressing from behind. The shouting became deafening. Faces reddened and twisted with rage.

The commander had Paul hauled inside the barracks and the doors barred.

I ran for Luke. By the time we returned to the Roman barracks, the mob had been dispersed. I demanded to see the commander and told him Paul was a Roman citizen. He had us escorted to Paul.

He sat against the wall, badly bruised, his mouth split and bleeding. "At least I escaped a scourging."

Luke saw to his wounds. I put my hand gently on his shoulders, and saw even that touch caused him pain. "Everyone is praying." I had brought bread, almonds, raisin cakes, and watered wine.

Tears ran down his face. His shoulders slumped. "If only they would listen."

Luke spoke gently. "They did, for a while."

"The Lord gives them opportunity day after day, Paul. We will keep on praying and speak when we can. There are still many in Jerusalem who follow Christ, and the city has not been left to Ananias and his mob."

Luke shook his head. "The swelling will go down soon, Paul. But the blows may have worsened your eyesight."

The guard said we had to leave.

Paul sighed. "Perhaps these Roman guards will listen."

That made me smile.

The commander took Paul to the high council, and we heard Paul divided them by proclaiming he was on trial for believing in resurrection. The debate between Pharisees and Sadducees became so heated and disorderly, that the Roman soldiers took Paul under guard and returned him to the fortress.

I knew it would not end there. The city was in turmoil over Paul. Rumors flew about plots against his life. I prayed unceasingly.

The Lord reminded me that my friend was destined to go to Rome.

When I went to tell him, the Roman guard said, "He is not here."

"Where have they taken him?"

He refused to answer.

I went to Paul's sister. She had seen him. So had her son. "I heard some men talking in the Temple," the boy told me. "They'd joined others in a plot to kill my uncle. They said they would fast from food and drink until he's dead. There are forty of them, Silas! I went and told Paul, and he told me to tell the officer in charge."

We made inquiries and soon learned two hundred soldiers under the command of two centurions had left Jerusalem the night before. "I have a friend among the soldiers," one of the brethren said. "And he told me seventy horsemen and two hundred spearmen went with them."

"And Paul?"

"He couldn't say for sure, only that they had a prisoner in chains and were taking him to Caesarea to the Roman governor."

I laughed. "Even the Roman army bends to the Lord's will and protects God's chosen servant!"

Luke left immediately for Caesarea, but one crisis after another kept me in Jerusalem.

"The high priest has gone to Caesarea," James told me. "And he's taken Tertullus with him."

"Tertullus might be famous for arguing Jewish and Roman

law, but all the forces Satan can muster will not prevail against the Lord's plans for Paul."

+ + +

Luke wrote to me, and I kept the council apprised of Paul's well-being and state of mind. By the time I was able to make the journey to see him, Ananias, the Jewish leaders, and Tertullus had long since failed in their attempts to sway Governor Felix into handing Paul over to them. In truth, I think Felix enjoyed aggravating them. He was a freed slave from Emperor Claudius's household, and ambitious. He married Drusilla, the great-granddaughter of the infamous King Herod the Great, thinking the alliance would commend him favorably to the Jews. It did not. The Herodians are hated for their Idumean blood. His marriage merely mixed it more.

Paul looked well, but I knew imprisonment chafed him. He could only preach to few.

"Ah, Silas, you are a friend who knows me." Paul grasped my arms in greeting, much pleased at the writing supplies I had brought him. "I have a dozen letters to answer and had no means to do so."

"Has there been any indication yet what the governor plans to do with you?"

"Nothing. He calls for me and I tell him about Jesus. I live in hope he will listen."

I stayed a few weeks and wrote letters he dictated, then returned to Jerusalem. I went back to Caesarea after Passover and found Paul frustrated.

"The governor finds me entertaining!" He paced, wretched with impatience. "He hopes in vain for a bribe. Had I money to offer, I would not!"

Governor Felix's heart proved to be hard.

"Why does God leave me here?"

"To refine you, perhaps, for a time when you will meet and speak to another far greater: Caesar."

He prayed all the time, not for himself, but for the churches he had planted. He is the only man I have ever known who could remember names, hundreds of them, and the circumstances of each person's salvation. His love grew and could not be bound within those stone walls. Prayer gave his love wings. He wrote countless letters, some to me, though they are gone now, passed on to others or burned by enemies. Those in my possession will survive. I have made copies to leave behind. Paul spoke words from the Lord, instructions and counsel to the congregations struggling against Satan, who will never cease to prowl. We must trust in the Lord, His Word, and the power of His strength to overcome, to endure to the end.

I thought some change would come when Rome recalled Felix. Judea made a man's career, or destroyed him. When later I came to Rome, I heard Felix had been banished in disgrace, and saw it an apt end for a man who left Paul in prison for no other reason than to please his enemies. Perhaps in exile, Felix's heart will soften.

Porcius Festus became governor. He came up to Jerusalem and was greeted by the chief priests and leading men of Jerusalem. They had not forgotten Paul, and asked the governor to have him brought to the city and put on trial. Festus did not give in to their demands. He courted Jewish favor to keep the peace, but did not relinquish any of his power. He said if the Jews had charges against Paul, they must come to Caesarea and make them before the Roman tribunal.

Before Festus left Jerusalem, the Lord gave me a vision of what was to come, and I went immediately to Caesarea.

"Under no circumstances must you agree to return to Jerusalem for trial, Paul."

"I will go where I am led."

"If you return to Jerusalem, it is not God leading you, but Satan! Listen to me! Their purpose is not to put you on trial, but to kill you on the way. You will be silenced."

"Christ will never be silenced."

"If you will not take into account my vision, remember what the Lord told you years ago. You will speak before kings! Stand firm, my friend, and the Lord will keep you to the course. You will testify before Caesar!"

When Festus ordered him to stand before the Jews and answer their charges, Paul called upon his right under Roman law to be heard. When Festus asked if he would be willing to return to Jerusalem, Paul refused. "I appeal to Caesar!"

Festus and his advisers quickly agreed, no doubt grateful to pass along responsibility for so troublesome a prisoner. Festus may have thought sending Paul away would assure some peace in Jerusalem.

King Agrippa and Bernice, his sister, came to Caesarea to pay their respects to the new Roman governor. Festus honored them with an elaborate ceremony and brought Paul out to speak before the king.

One of our Roman brethren told me, "He challenged Agrippa as a man might challenge a friend. Paul asked if he believed in the Jewish prophets. I know nothing of these things, but the king was disturbed by the questions Paul raised. He left the room. Festus and Bernice went with him. I was told Paul might have been set free if he hadn't appealed to Caesar."

Soon after, I received a letter from Luke.

"The governor has given orders for Paul to be taken under guard to Rome. Can you accompany us?"

I longed to go with them and prayed fervently that God would allow me to do so. I spoke with the others on the council and we all prayed about it. None had peace about letting me go, though they sent me to Caesarea to bless Paul and bring him provisions.

He wept when he saw me. He must have seen in my face that I could not go. "I knew it was too much to ask, but I hoped . . ."

"I'm needed here, for now, at least. When do you leave?"

"Within the week." He grasped my arms. "We worked well together, my friend. Think of all those thousands from Antioch to Athens and back again." He sighed. "I wish you were coming with me. I could have used your help."

I tried to soften his disappointment and my own. "You've written a few good letters without me."

He laughed.

What little time we had together, we used to write letters.

I saw him off. It was a difficult parting. We thought we would never see each other again.

But as I have learned over the years, God always seems to have other plans.

SOMEONE cleared his throat. Silas turned.

Epanetus crossed his arms and leaned against the door-frame. "I have never seen a man so dedicated to a task." He searched Silas's face. "I did not intend to add to your grief."

"I have more good memories than bad, Epanetus." Silas smiled wistfully. "When Paul sailed from Caesarea, I never thought to see him again."

"You've lost many friends."

Silas rose from the writing table. "As have we all." He stretched. "Thankfully, they are not lost to us forever."

The Roman smiled. "The Lord is renewing your faith."

"Even a dog gets tired of licking its wounds."

"Patrobas said word has spread that you're here. Many have asked to come. Do you feel up to teaching?"

Teaching was second nature to Silas, but he feared that the larger gathering might endanger this small congregation. He voiced his concerns. "Perhaps I should move soon."

"I've lived with danger all my life, Silas, but never with a greater purpose than now. But I leave it to you." He chuckled. "Curiatus is especially eager to speak with you. The boy has come every day that you've been here. He knocked at my door again this morning."

"He reminds me of Timothy." Silas thought of Diana and wondered what life would have been like to have a wife and children and why this longing came now when it was past hope.

"What do you say?"

"Say about what?"

"I wonder at your reverie, Silas." Epanetus seemed amused. "Shall I send word to Diana that she may bring Curiatus?"

Silas turned away and fiddled with the reed pens. "Just send for the boy."

Curiatus came, and Silas spent an hour answering his questions before the others arrived for the meeting.

People sat close together to make space for everyone. Silas looked into their eager faces—strangers most of them, yet all bound together by love of Jesus.

"I heard the Lord speak in Galilee," he said. "He stood on a boat a little way from shore while thousands sat on the hillside listening. His voice carried to where I stood on the edge of the crowd, above them." He smiled wryly. "I did not understand all of what He said, but what I did disturbed me greatly. His words went into me like a sword, cutting through all the notions I had about who I was and what I was meant to do with my life. To follow Him, I would have to change everything. That frightened me. So I left."

Resting his forearms on his knees, Silas leaned forward and clasped his hands in front of him. He could not see their faces through his tears. "I look back and see how many opportunities the Lord gave me, how often I knew His words were directed at the sin that held me captive, how long it took before I let Him remove all the traps that kept me caged." He covered his face. "Oh, what fools we can be, holding tight to the things of this world and believing they are our salvation."

"But you let go, Silas. You gave your life to Christ. You wouldn't be here with us now if you hadn't."

Curiatus with his compassionate heart. Timothy all over

again. Silas lowered his hands. "I can't tell you I haven't struggled or thought of what my life might have been." He looked at Diana. "Or what I gave up."

Her expression softened. "We all struggle, Silas." Her mouth curved so gently. "Each day has its trials to face."

"Yes." He sighed. "Each day is a struggle to hold tight to faith." Especially when one saw men and women executed for following Jesus' teaching to love God, love one another, and treat everyone with compassion, mercy, and truth, even when it would not be returned in kind. "Jesus told us not to worry about tomorrow, for tomorrow will bring its own worries. Today's trouble is enough for today, as we all well know. Jesus tells us to seek the Kingdom of God above all else, and live righteously, and He will give you everything you need. I saw Jesus. I heard Him speak. But you, here with me now . . . Your work will always be to have faith in what you have not seen with your own eyes, to trust in the testimony of men like Peter and Paul and John Mark."

"And you," Diana said. "We trust in your word, Silas."

His throat tightened. He could not hold her gaze.

"The world is Satan's battlefield, but if we live in Christ, we live victorious through His death and resurrection. To believe is the hardest work of all when the world stands shoulder to shoulder against you."

"I've heard Christians say there never was a resurrection."

Silas glanced up sharply and saw Urbanus standing back. "I assure you Jesus lives."

"And what of the reports that Jesus' body was hidden so that the disciples might make false claims about his resurrection?"

"It is not a new claim, Urbanus." Silas shook his head.

"Those rumors have circulated for years. The Jewish leaders paid the guards at the tomb to spread them. I might've believed them had I not seen Jesus for myself. But I and the disciples were only some of the many who saw Jesus. He spoke to hundreds of His followers. He spent forty days with us *after* He arose from the tomb, teaching us and preparing us to go out and make the truth known: that we all can be reconciled to God through Him. Later, He appeared to Paul." He spread his hands and shrugged. "The world will always lie about Jesus."

"And hate those who follow Him," Epanetus said.

"If only He had stayed with us, the world would know."

Silas smiled. "Someday, at the name of Jesus every knee will bow and every tongue confess that Jesus Christ is Lord."

Curiatus looked back at the others. "Miracles are proof."

Diana put her hand on her son's knee. "Miracles don't sway people. Remember Silas telling us about the ten lepers Jesus healed? Only one went back to thank Him."

Epanetus agreed. "It wouldn't matter if five hundred witnesses of Christ's resurrection testified in a court of law. The fact is, my friends, some will refuse to believe, and no amount of evidence will ever sway them."

Silas felt their dejection. He had felt little hope when he came here. Yet, the weeks and work of remembering had helped renew him enough to give them some encouragement.

"The proof is in this room." He looked around slowly at each of them. "When Christ comes in, we change." He smiled, his heart lifting as he thought of others he had known. "I've seen thieves become honorable and generous. I've known temple prostitutes who married and now live as faithful husbands and wives. I've seen homosexuals become chaste servants of God."

"Even so, Silas," Patrobas said bleakly, "don't you long for heaven? Don't you long for an end to the suffering? for the fear to be over?"

Silas let out his breath softly. He stared down at his clasped hands before speaking. "Every day over the past months, I've asked the Lord why I'm left behind when all but a handful of friends have gone on to be with Him." He looked into the faces of those listening. "I'm not alone in those feelings. Life is a struggle. Even in the best of times, it's a battle to live for Jesus in this fallen world." Hadn't he felt the emptiness and vanity of life when he had everything a man could want? "It would be a relief for anyone to accept Christ one day and be caught up into heaven with Him the next."

There was a soft twittering of laughter.

Oh, Lord, I have lived like a man without strength for too long. Help me speak what I know is true, and heal my angry, doubting heart.

He brought them back to earth. "But what of the lost?" He smiled sadly. "Remember. Jesus called us the salt of the earth. Our presence preserves life and gives others time to know the truth. The Lord will come when God decides. For now, we hold fast to faith. We cling to Jesus' promises in the midst of tribulation."

Sometimes the tribulation came from within the body of Christ. He and Paul and Peter had written countless letters to the churches, warning them against false teaching, encouraging believers to turn back and follow Jesus' example. *Love others! Live for what is right! Live pure and blameless lives! Be faithful!*

Tribulation came from losing sight of Jesus and looking at the troubled, fallen world. Peter walked on water until he took his eyes off Jesus.

Everyone in the room sat silent, the only sound the water splashing from the fountain.

"I came to you broken in spirit and struggling in faith. The world is a sea of despair, and I was drowning in it. I have said words to you that I'd forgotten." He looked up at Epanetus standing in the corner. "Thank you for making me remember."

———————————— ✦   ✦   ✦ ————————————

WHEN *I returned to Jerusalem, the council gave me a letter from Peter, who had gone north to Antioch to encourage the church there. I struggled to read Peter's writing. He had taken his wife and several traveling companions. Now, we learned he had sent four of those companions north—two to preach in Cappadocia, while two others traveled farther to reach Parnassus in Galatia. Peter intended to visit the churches in Pamphylia and Phrygia, travel on to Ephesus, then sail to Rome. Several men from Antioch had offered to go with him, but Peter said they were needed in Syria. I felt a fillip at those words.*

"I leave on the new moon and pray the Lord will provide me with a companion who can write in Hebrew, Greek, and Latin. Jesus called me a fisher of men, but never a man of letters."

I could almost see Peter's self-deprecating smile, and chuckled. "He needs a secretary."

"Yes. He does."

James's tone made me look up. He smiled at me. "Paul and Peter in Rome. Think of it, Silas."

I caught his excitement. "The Lord aims at the very heart of the empire."

"Who will we send?" another asked.

"Someone must go and help Peter."

From the moment I read the first few lines, I had known what the Lord wanted of me. Smiling, I rolled the scroll and held it like a baton. "Send me."

And so they did.

I took John Mark with me.

+   +   +

I sold the last of my reserves, accepted the help of others within the body of Christ, and headed north. We all knew Peter could be impetuous. He might not wait. When I arrived and was brought to him, I saw I had barely reached Antioch in time. "Oh, ye of little patience," I said, grinning.

Peter had finished packing. He turned to me with a laugh. "Silas! I dared not hope!"

We embraced. Though much older than I, he still was the stronger. A look of relief came into his wife's face. "God is kind to send you with my husband."

I kissed her cheek. "I am the more blessed."

Peter slapped me hard on the back.

I laughed. It was good to see him. Of all the disciples, Peter remained my favorite. The first time he told me he had denied Jesus three times before the Lord was crucified, I knew we had much in common.

"We leave for Tarsus in the morning," Peter told me.

"Will you allow Silas so little time to rest, Peter?"

"We have little time, beloved. Besides, I grow older by the day."

Old, perhaps, but robust. He was twenty-five years older

than I, and I was hard-pressed to keep up with him. There were days when I longed for sunset so that he would stop and I could rest!

His wife managed without apparent difficulty. "The Lord has given me fifty years to learn to keep pace with him, Silas." She even managed to prepare meals when we camped!

I never tired of listening to Peter talk about Jesus. Who could speak with more authority than one who had been among the first to be called? Jesus had lived in Peter's house in Capernaum. Peter had seen his mother-in-law healed of a debilitating fever. He had seen Jesus turn water into wine at a wedding in Cana. Peter had been on the mountain when Moses and Elijah appeared and spoke to Jesus. Peter had seen Jesus as He truly was: God the Son, the Light of the world. God had revealed Jesus as Messiah to this humble, oft-stubborn, hot-tempered fisherman. Peter had been in the garden of Gethsemane, where Jesus prayed in preparation for His crucifixion. While others fled into the night, Peter had followed after Jesus and the mob that arrested Him, staying close enough to see Him interrogated. Peter had listened to Mary Magdalene, and entered the empty tomb. And he had been in the upper room with the disciples when Jesus came and proved death had no power over Him.

Before the Lord ascended, He commissioned Peter to "feed My sheep." And while doing so, Peter never lost sight of his weakness. He always spoke freely of his failings.

"Jesus asked me to pray, and I fell asleep during His hours of greatest need. When Jesus was arrested, I tried to kill Malchus," a fellow brother now, and one of those who had traveled north with Peter. I had heard them joke about Peter's bad aim.

"I denied even knowing Jesus, not once, but three times."

Tears often streamed down his cheeks when he spoke. "Jesus called me *Petros*, 'the rock,' and my faith was sand. And still He loved me, as He loves you. He forgave me, as He has forgiven you. He restored me, and will restore you. Jesus asked me three times if I loved Him, once for each time I denied Him. Jesus knows us better than we know ourselves. . . ."

I wondered at times why there were no riots in the cities we visited, few attempts to murder Peter. He spoke the same message Paul did and with the power of the Holy Spirit. Yet, the Jews paid no attention to him. I can only surmise the Jewish leaders thought a fisherman beneath contempt. Paul was a scholar; Peter was not. Paul had been one of their own, even one elevated in stature by his intellect and training under Gamaliel, the grandson of Hillel, to whom only the best and brightest could apply. Peter had been trained by Jesus, the One who opened the gate to all willing to come into His fold.

Thousands came to know Jesus through Peter's testimony. I saw the light come into the eyes of so many.

As we traveled the same route Paul and I had taken, I saw and was able to introduce dear friends. Aquila and Priscilla opened their home to us in Ephesus. Timothy and I spent precious hours together. He missed Paul, but had become an able leader. He loved Paul like a father, and grieved deeply over his imprisonment. "I fear he will die in Rome."

And so he would. I knew at the time, but did not tell Timothy lest his confidence be crushed. He still worried he was not up to the task Paul had given him.

"Paul would not have sent you back to Ephesus to deal with difficulties among these believers if he had not had confidence in your faith and ability to teach. Hold fast to what you know, Timothy. Do you remember what Paul taught you?"

"He taught me many things."

"And what did he say about Scripture?"

"It is inspired by God and is useful to teach us what is true and to make us realize what is wrong in our lives. It corrects us when we are wrong and teaches us to do what is right."

"And through the Scriptures, God prepares and equips His people to do every good work."

"Yes," Peter said, "but remember, too, my friends, it is not you who saves. It is the Lord who captures the heart. Unless the Lord calls someone, they will not come."

"I am learning that every day," Timothy said bleakly. "My words often fail to convince—"

"Your work is to believe, my son." Peter spoke firmly. "And testify to the truth of Christ. Jesus is the only begotten Son of God, crucified for our sins, buried three days, and raised. You teach that, and the Holy Spirit will do the rest."

Peter spoke in simple words, and God used them to crack open the hardest hearts.

Yet, still, I have learned that it is not in the nature of some men to allow God to do the work. People—even those with the best of intentions—try to save others by their own strength, thinking their words can persuade and change hearts. They often find themselves disciplined by God. I pray Timothy never went down that path.

We sailed from Ephesus. Peter stood at the helm, savoring his time on the sea, while I groaned for the feel of land beneath my feet. We arrived safely in Greece and met with Apollos.

Men were often in awe of Peter, and he knew how to put them quickly at ease. He revealed his frailties and failures. "We are all ordinary men who serve an extraordinary God."

Priscilla and Aquila had sent their greetings to Apollos.

"I am indebted to Priscilla and Aquila," Apollos said. "They had courage enough to take me aside and correct my teaching. I knew nothing of the Holy Spirit."

I laughed. "Priscilla is like a mother hen."

Apollos grinned. "Indeed, she is. She took me under her wing rather firmly."

Corinth was beset with problems.

"So many turn back to their old habits." Apollos sought Peter's advice. "The people can't seem to break away from sin."

"Without God, it is impossible. Even those who have accepted Christ and received the Holy Spirit contend with the sin nature. I battle natural inclinations every day." Peter slapped Apollos on the shoulder. "The problem, my young friend, is not how to break the chains—God has already done that—but the willingness to enslave ourselves to Jesus, who sets us free."

"A great paradox."

"Our faith is full of paradoxes. It takes the mind of Christ to understand." Peter laughed. "That's why the Lord had to give us the Holy Spirit. So we could understand."

While the Lord promised peace of mind and heart to believers, the Christian life is a constant battleground, for the world is set against God. We also struggle with the power of sin. We fight against sinful desires. We war against our selfishness. Even when we do good, pride tries to steal glory from God. One paradox after another. The only way to win is to lay down our arms. The only way to live is to die, to give up our life to Christ. Jesus is the only victor, and only by surrendering completely to Him do we share that victory.

Peter said it more simply. "Trust in the Lord and the power of His strength. . . ."

The church leaders gathered daily, plying him with questions, and the once hotheaded, impetuous fisherman spoke with the patience of the Master.

The oft-asked question: "How do we avoid persecution?"

Peter said, "Jesus did not avoid crucifixion. He gave up His life for our sake, and calls us to do the same for others." He never wasted words. "Trials will show that your faith is genuine. Be glad when persecuted. Instead of asking to avoid it, ask for the strength to endure."

Believers walked with us over the Corinthian isthmus. Peter used every moment to teach. "We are one body, together in Christ. Nothing can separate us. Think clearly in the midst of tribulation. Exercise control. The Lord has given us the ability to restrain ourselves. Don't complain. Live as God's obedient children. Don't slip back into your old ways. Remember, the heavenly Father to whom you pray does not have favorites. He will judge or reward you according to what you do. Believe in Him and behave in a way pleasing to the Lord."

Before we boarded the ship, he gathered them close. "Hold fast to your faith, children. Live your life in reverent fear of the Lord, who loves you and sent His Son to die for your sins. Rid yourselves of evil and show sincere love for each other. Pray. . . ."

I longed to unfurl a scroll and write his words down, but had not the opportunity then. But I remember now. He dictated short, beautiful letters, copies of which I keep with me. The words they contain are my shield of hope against arrows of doubt. I tell you, whenever Peter spoke, his words came like pearls from God's treasure box.

"If we die with Him . . ." he said.

They responded as we had taught them. "We will also live with Him."

"If we endure hardship . . ."

"We will reign with Him."

"If we are unfaithful . . ."

"He remains faithful, for He cannot deny who He is."

Peter embraced and kissed them one by one as he had kissed his own children good-bye, trusting God to protect and guide them in the difficult days ahead.

I often think of Apollos, Aquila and Priscilla, and so many others I met along the road.

And I pray for them, knowing, if they live, they still pray for me.

+   +   +

We had hoped to board a ship destined for Rome, but ended up sailing to Tarentum instead. Perhaps I became used to sailing, for the journey across the Savonic Gulf did not leave me a huddled mass beside a putrid basin in the belly of the ship, or hanging over the stern. I even joined Peter at the bow, though I had cause to think better of it later. When the ship dipped, a wave splashed up over me and had not Peter grasped hold of my belt, I would have slid down the deck and underfoot of working sailors. His laughter boomed. How I loved that man! He was so unlike the scholarly men I had known, and yet, like a father.

I have not been on the sea since that voyage, but when I stand by the window here in Puteoli, and smell the salt sea air, I think of Peter and his wife. Not as they died, but as they lived, and live still in the presence of the Lord. All pain and suffering is over.

For them.

Before we reached land, Peter had become acquainted with every sailor aboard our ship. He knew wind and sails, and they knew he was one of them—a man of the sea. When his Galilean accent proved too difficult for some, I translated. He told them sea stories: the flood and Noah's ark! Moses parting the Red Sea! Jonah swallowed by a huge fish! the stormy Sea of Tiberias and God the Son, Jesus, who walked on water! Jesus, crucified, buried, raised, offered life eternal to anyone who believed.

As we neared Tarentum, Juno, the first mate, came to Peter. "I have decided to give up the sea for the Lord. As soon as we reach port, I will ask Asyncritis to release me and go to Rome with you."

Peter put his arm around him and faced him out to sea. "I told you of the fierce gale when we were on the Sea of Galilee and how Jesus slept? how we awakened Him, and He commanded the wind and sea to hush and be still?"

"Yes."

Peter put his hands on the rail. "We crossed to the country of the Gerasenes. No sooner had we come out of the boat than we saw a wild man running out from among the tombs. He came toward us. He had been chained and shackled there numerous times, but nothing could hold him. I was much younger then, and far stronger than I am now, but I feared the man would do harm to Jesus. He screamed curses at us and frothed at the mouth. When he picked up stones, I thought he meant to hurl them at us. Instead, he gashed himself until his arms and legs streamed blood. Jesus said, 'Come out of the man, you evil spirit.' Just a few words, quietly spoken as the man ran toward us. I thought the demoniac meant to attack Jesus, and I got in his way." He gave a self-deprecating laugh. "I often put myself in front of Jesus. You see, I still didn't understand who He was."

Peter gripped Juno's arm. "Jesus took hold of me and

stepped past. He went out to meet the demoniac." His voice roughened. "The man fell to his knees and bowed down, crying out, 'I beg you, don't torture me!' His name was Legion. That's how many demons lived in him!" He let go of Juno. "They spoke. We were all terrified of him. Voice after voice came from that wretched man, pleading with Jesus not to send them to some distant place. The demons knew who Jesus was and from where He had come. Jesus cast them out after they asked permission to enter a herd of pigs feeding on mountain grasses."

He leaned his hip against the rail and looked at Juno. "The herdsmen saw everything just as we did and ran away. They brought the townspeople back. We had bathed the man, by then, and baptized him. Nathanael had given him a tunic and belt, John a robe. When the townspeople all saw him in his right mind, they were even more afraid. They begged Jesus to leave the Ten Towns and go away."

"Fools, all of them!"

"Do not be so quick to judge, Juno. Some are not ready to accept Jesus the first time they meet Him."

I knew the truth of that only too well.

"Did Jesus say or do anything to change their mind?"

Peter smiled. "No. He got into the boat."

"And set sail?"

"Yes."

The sudden flap of a sail made Juno glance up sharply. He barked an order; several sailors moved quickly to do his bidding. He returned his attention to Peter. "Jesus took the man with Him."

"No. He didn't. The man begged to come with us. Jesus told him to go home and tell everyone what great things the Lord had done for him. 'Tell them how merciful God has been.'"

Juno scowled. "You said Jesus called men to follow Him."

"Yes, Juno, but sometimes following means staying where you are." Peter put his hand on Juno's arm and smiled. "Remain as first mate on this fine ship. Serve your captain as you would serve the Lord. Wherever you are bound, God goes with you. What you carry now within you is precious cargo, cargo more precious than all the gold in the empire. *The Good News of Jesus Christ*. Carry it to distant shores. Spread the Word among all those you meet. Remember what Jesus said to the demoniac: 'Tell them everything the Lord has done for you and how merciful he has been.'"

"I understand," Juno said grimly, "but I would rather go with you and Silas."

"Ah, yes, and I would rather be with the Lord." He spread his arms. "But here we are—you, me, my wife, Silas—all of us servants of the Lord who saved us and called us to Himself. We do His will, not our own."

We stayed in Tarentum a few weeks, during which Peter met often with Juno. Two other sailors came with him. Peter blessed Juno before we left. "The Lord is your captain."

We followed the road over the mountains. While resting in Pompeii, we spoke to people in the agora. Then we headed north for Rome.

Word spread of Peter's arrival, and Jewish believers came to see him. Some of them had been in Jerusalem during Pentecost when the Holy Spirit had come, and were among the three thousand saved.

There was no word of Paul.

Rome is both magnificent and depraved, a towering achievement of man's efforts and limitless vanities. We found our way around the city easily and learned many things from the Jews who had returned from exile after Emperor Claudius's death. Some said Agrippina poisoned her husband soon after he adopted her son Nero. Britannicus, natural son of Claudius and his heir, died mysteriously during a dinner party, leaving Agrippina to rule. She did so, later declaring Nero emperor of Rome. Many knew she held the reins of power. Roman coins bore her likeness facing Nero, signifying their equality.

Letters arrived from Puteoli. Paul had arrived in Italy under Roman guard, after he and Luke had spent three months on the island of Malta, where they had been shipwrecked. "He will stay at the Forum on the Appian Way and then at The Three Taverns. . . ."

John Mark and I hastened to meet them, and I was filled with joy at the sight of them. Laughing, Paul embraced me. "I did not think I would see you again! And here you are in Rome ahead of us. And John Mark!" He embraced the young man, their misunderstanding long since put to rest.

"I understand you had quite a voyage." John Mark grinned.

"A long, dark, wet voyage, but filled with opportunity!" He introduced us to Julius, the Roman officer in charge of him, and then greeted the others who had come with me. Luke and I talked. His first concern was Paul's health.

"Julius said Paul can have his own lodgings while he awaits trial. Can you arrange for this, Silas?"

"Yes. Peter knows several people who can secure lodgings for you both." I smiled. "So, Paul made a believer of his guard!"

"Julius has not said so directly, but he has the greatest respect for Paul, and God has used him mightily in protecting our friend from harm. When the ship wrecked within sight of shore, the other soldiers wanted to execute all the prisoners so their lives wouldn't be forfeit if any escaped. But for Paul's sake, Julius ordered them all spared."

Luke explained how Paul had warned the ship's captain from the onset of the voyage that they would be shipwrecked and all cargo lost. "No one would listen. We ran before a northeastern storm for days. We couldn't see the stars, so there was no way to know where we were going."

They had lightened the ship by casting the cargo overboard, and then some of the gear as well.

"Some feared we would end up shipwrecked on the African coast. In truth, Silas, I thought we would die. Only Paul had hope. God had told him he would stand trial before Caesar, not that any man aboard believed him. The ship hung up between two rocks. We could see a beach. Those who could swim to shore did so. The rest of us clung to whatever floated. I drank my share of seawater. So did Paul."

"How were you received on Malta?"

"Very well. It was cold and raining. The people built a fire on the shore. A poisonous snake bit Paul, and he shook it off into the fire." He chuckled. "The people thought he must be a murderer and justice would prevail. They sat around watching and waiting for Paul to die. When he didn't, they thought he was a god and took us to Publius, who honored us even more when Paul healed his father. The man was dying of dysentery. Malta brought their sick to Paul, and he healed them." He shook his head. "I've often wondered why he cannot heal himself of his impaired vision and the infection that plagues him."

"He told me once those things keep him dependent upon God's strength."

I sent word ahead to Rome. Paul wanted to meet with Peter and then as many Jewish leaders as would come.

Within days of his arrival, the Jewish leaders filled Paul's rented house to hear what he had to say.

"I am bound with this chain because I believe that the hope of Israel—the Messiah—has already come."

They shook their heads. "We have had no letters from Judea or reports against you from anyone who has come here. The only thing we know about this movement is that it is denounced everywhere."

What they said was true. We had been denounced by many whose hearts had become so hard that no seed of truth could be planted. Jews as well as Gentiles. We prayed constantly that we would have time to spread the Good News in Rome, for all roads led to the great city. Those same roads would carry Christians to every province in the world.

Another meeting was set. Many more came to hear Paul. He preached from morning through the day and into evening, offering proof from the five books of Moses and the Prophets.

When he finished, the Jewish leaders rose. "We will discuss the matter among ourselves."

I despaired at those lukewarm words. I knew those who believed at that moment had not the strength of faith to come back and hear more. The others stood stiff-necked with pride, rejecting the idea that the Messiah would choose to die rather than call upon angelic forces to purge Israel of its Roman oppressors. They wanted nothing less than that their Messiah restore their kingdom as it had been under Solomon's reign. They wanted King David, the warrior, not King Jesus, Prince of Peace.

Paul rose, too, face flushed, eyes blazing.

"The Holy Spirit was right when he said to your ancestors, 'The hearts of these people are hardened, and their ears cannot hear, and they have closed their eyes. . . .'"

They bristled.

He calmed, but still spoke bold truth with no hint of compromise. "I want you to know that this salvation from God has also been offered to the Gentiles, and *they will accept it.*"

They left. From the beginning, the Scriptures proclaimed Jesus Lord over *all* the earth. All those who turned to Him would be accepted. God told our father Abraham that he would be a blessing to others, that all the families of the earth would be blessed through him. The Messiah would come through the Jews.

If only they would receive Him . . .

I often weep for my people. I pray they will turn their hearts back to God. And I will continue to pray for that as long as I have breath.

Of course, Paul continued to receive and teach in the house we rented for him. He welcomed all who came to visit, spoke the truth and won many to Christ, including Julius, who was eventually reassigned to another post, we knew not where. We prayed for him daily, that the Lord would protect him. A fire started, and a large section of Rome burned. Roman guards came with orders to move Paul to the emperor's dungeon. We knew the end was near.

Nero reigned like a petulant child, ordering the death of anyone he suspected of plotting against him. He had his own mother, Agrippina, executed; though I saw this as a just ending for a woman as wicked as King Ahab's wife, Jezebel, who led so many astray by idol worship. She made her murdered husband, Claudius, into a god, and herself his high priestess, though the cult fast became a joke in Rome once she was dead.

Seneca and Burrus are dead, and with them any hope of justice. Nero now listens to the counsel of Tigellinus, who has revived the treason law. Many Roman nobles have been executed on suspicion of conspiracy against the emperor. No one is safe. Even Octavia, Nero's cast-aside wife of noble blood, has been executed, while his new empress, Poppaea, fans his growing vanity.

The proverb holds true: "When evil sits upon the throne, good people hide."

Only Christians have the assurance of heaven.

The emperor cast blame on the Christians for the fire because Paul and Peter prophesied the judgment will come with fire in the end. Some say Nero ordered it himself, to clear the way for his plans to rebuild Rome and call it Neropolis. Only God knows who did it and why, but we suffer for it. We are hunted down. We are bound to arena columns, doused with pitch, and set on fire to serve as torches for Nero's games.

We suffer the loss of those we love.

Paul is beheaded. I have the coat he sent to me, a cherished gift from the Jerusalem council.

Peter and his wife are crucified.

Hundreds are in hiding, meeting in caves and holding fast to their faith in darkness.

Luke left Rome.

This world is not my home. Each day I live in it, I struggle. I remind myself that the battle is won, the victory is secure, and my life safe in the hands of Jesus, who will bring me home to heaven. And still, every day is a struggle to hold fast to that which I know to be true.

Oh, how I long for the day when Christ will call me home and this war within me will be over!

But I know this now in this quiet room in Puteoli: the Lord has left me here for a purpose. I must go on. I must run the race Paul spoke of so often. My friend reached the finish line and wears the laurel wreath. I imagine him now, sitting in the stadium of heaven, cheering me on.

For Peter, life was a voyage, the Holy Spirit propelling him across the sea. The Lord has brought him and his wife to safe harbor.

Those I loved most dearly are not lost, only beyond my sight.

I cannot give up!

I cannot fail!

I must go on!

SILAS put his reed pen aside and carefully cut the papyrus scroll so that none was wasted. He rolled the unused portion and tucked it into his pack. He blew on the last few letters he had written. They dried quickly. Removing the weights, he let his memories roll closed. With a deep sigh of satisfaction, he rested his elbows on the table and rubbed his face. The task Epanetus and the others had given him was finished.

Copies of Peter's letters had been sent to faithful friends in the five provinces of Asia, one to each elder trained by Paul. He had also made copies of Paul's letter to Roman Christians, giving one to Patrobas. "Take this north to John Mark. If he has left Rome, give the letter to Ampliatus. He will guard it with his life."

He made another copy for Epanetus. It would help him teach those under his care.

He had made copies of the letter Paul had asked him to write to all Hebrew Christians everywhere. He had fasted and prayed before writing it. The Lord revealed to him how the commandments, the rituals, and the prophets presented God's promises and showed the path to forgiveness and salvation through Jesus Christ, the long-awaited Messiah. He knew well the struggle of the old faith and the new life in Christ, for he had lived it. He poured his heart into the letter, wanting all Jews to know Jesus was superior to angels, leaders, and priests. The old covenant was fulfilled in Christ, and the new had given them freedom in Christ. The sanctuary was no longer the Temple in Jerusalem, for the Lord now dwelled within the heart of everyone who accepted Him as Savior and Lord. Christ, the perfect sacrifice, had set them free. The letter commanded brothers and sisters to hold fast to their new faith, encourage one another, and look forward to Christ's return. And it gave them instructions on how to live godly lives.

Paul had read the letter and given him a satisfied smile. "Well written, my friend!"

High praise, indeed, from a man Silas greatly admired. But he could take no credit. "The Lord gave me the words."

"Of that, Silas, I have no doubt."

How Silas missed talking to Paul about the Word of the Lord. He missed Paul's passion, his dedication, his perseverance. He had been honored to watch Paul grow more humble over time, and had seen him near the end so filled with love and compassion that it spilled from him as it had from Christ. Paul's touch healed many; his words rang with truth. God, in His infinite wisdom, had chosen an enemy and made him into a most intimate friend.

Silas laid out the scrolls before him. His life's work. He would not part with any of them, but would continue to guard the original letters Paul had dictated, and those he had helped Peter write, along with the one he had written but left unsigned. He weighed Paul's letter to the Romans in one hand while holding several smaller scrolls in the other, smiling at the difference. Paul, the scholar, could not say anything in less than a few hours, while Peter, the fisherman, could speak the wisdom of the ages in a few minutes. Both had confounded the greatest minds in the empire, for the wisdom of this world is foolishness to God.

Anguish and joy welled up in him. Clutching the scrolls against his chest, Silas bowed his head, tears of gratitude flowing down his cheeks. "Oh, Lord, that You would allow me such privilege . . ."

How few had been given the opportunity to travel with one, let alone two great men of God. The Lord had placed Silas at Paul's side when he had gone out to spread the Good News to the Greeks, and then, beside Peter when he made the long journey to Rome. He had served as secretary to each. He had walked thousands of miles with Paul, and sailed with Peter. He had seen both men perform miracles. He had helped them establish churches. They had been his friends.

". . . that You would use me, the least deserving . . ."

I chose you. I formed your inner parts and knit you together in your mother's womb. You are Mine.

"May it always be so, Lord. Search me and know my heart. Test me and know my anxious thoughts. Point out anything in me that offends You, and lead me along the path of everlasting life."

He carefully arranged the scrolls so that none would be damaged when carried. He left one on the table. He would read it tonight when everyone met.

He felt a great burden lift from him. He had been cloistered far too long. It was time to go for a walk outside the walls of Epanetus's fortress home.

Macombo stood in the courtyard, holding a pitcher.

"Tell Epanetus the task is finished."

Macombo straightened from watering a plant. "You look better than I've seen you."

"Yes." Faith restored, he felt healed of affliction. "I'm going outside to see Puteoli. It's about time, isn't it?" He laughed. "I'll be back before the meeting."

Silas wandered the streets all afternoon. He talked with

strangers and lingered at the port. The sea air brought a flood of memories.

"Silas?"

His heart took a fillip at the familiar voice. He turned, pulse racing. "Diana." She had a basket of fish on her hip. He looked for Curiatus. "Your son is not with you?" He never saw them apart.

"He's working. Over there. He's a diver." She pointed. "You can see him on the dock between those two ships."

Men shouted and Curiatus dove into the water. He came up next to a box floating near a ship and began securing a rope around it.

"He's a strong swimmer."

She had moved closer to him and looked up at him. "I've never seen you down here."

He felt lost in her gaze. "I haven't been outside the house since I arrived on Epanetus's doorstep." Embarrassed, he gave a soft laugh and looked away. Had he been staring? "I've been wandering since early this afternoon." He was an old fool. But he couldn't seem to help himself.

Her face lit up. "You've finished, haven't you?"

He nodded because he couldn't trust his voice. It would soon be time to leave. He'd never see her again. Why should that hurt so much? He hardly knew her. He had not allowed himself to get too close to anyone in Puteoli, least of all this beautiful widow.

"There's so much I want to know about you, Silas." She blushed and gave an embarrassed laugh. "I mean, we all want to hear your story." She turned as Curiatus shouted for the box to be raised. "My son has pressed you since first you arrived."

"He helped renew my faith, Diana." He should not have said her name.

"We all saw how you were suffering when you came to us."

"We all suffer."

"Some more than others. I never met Paul or Peter. I've never met anyone who walked with Jesus. Only you."

Silas winced inwardly. The old regret rose. "I didn't walk with Him. Not the way you mean. Only once and for a few miles along the road, after He arose." He could not look at her for fear of the disappointment he might see in her beautiful, dark eyes. "I must go back." He smiled over her head. "I wouldn't want Epanetus to think I've run away again."

Macombo answered the door at the first knock. "Thank God! Come. Epanetus is pacing."

"There you are!" The Roman strode through the courtyard. "You've been gone long enough to reach Pompeii!" He said nothing about Diana.

"I left the scrolls."

"And finished the one everyone has been waiting to hear. I saw it." Epanetus's concern seemed unusually grave.

"What's happened?"

"Things have changed." Nero had widened the search for Christians. Some of the most honorable senators were dead now for no other reason than they were born of noble blood, executed by Tigellinus, the Sicilian upstart exiled by Emperor Caligula. "Tigellinus feeds Nero's vanity as well as his fears. If anyone falls asleep during one of Nero's performances, his life is forfeit! We can be thankful for one thing: an emperor who takes no time to rule his kingdom will not rule long."

Andronicus, Junia, Rufus, and his dear mother, who had all been so kind to Paul, had been martyred. "They are with the Lord now," Silas said.

"I would like to see the death of those who killed them!" Epanetus said fiercely.

Silas realized with some surprise that he felt no such hatred. "I do not wish death on any man unsaved."

Epanetus turned. "Even Nero?"

"Even him."

Epanetus considered him for a moment. "Julius told me Paul had great respect and affection for you. Paul told him you were a man of great intellect and compassion, a friend to him in all circumstances."

Silas felt the prick of tears at such words. "How did you come to know Paul's guard?"

"We served together in Judea before I fled."

"Fled?"

"Let's just say I made it out of Judea by the skin of my teeth and still keep an eye over my shoulder." He glanced around. "This house doesn't belong to me."

Silas resisted the desire to know more. "Where is Julius now?"

"I don't know. I haven't heard from him in weeks. Patrobas couldn't find him."

Silas feared he knew what that meant. "Are you in danger?"

"Not from Rome. Not yet, at least." The Roman relaxed somewhat, and beckoned. "Come. Have something to eat before the others arrive. You'll never have a chance otherwise."

"I must thank you for all you've done for me," Silas said, following him.

Epanetus snorted. "I feared I chained you to your desk."

"The task steadied me. When I came to your doorstep . . ." He shook his head. "I had little hope."

"I've known men whose minds broke with less provocation than you have had, my friend. All you needed was rest and time to remember."

✦   ✦   ✦

Silas read the scroll that evening, from beginning to end. When he rolled it closed, he knew there were many things he had left unsaid, things more important for them to know than about his life.

Had he made himself look good by writing only the best about himself? He knew he had. Diana sat close at his feet, Curiatus beside her. Those in Jerusalem had known everything about him. These two who had come to mean so much knew nothing.

"You said nothing of your family, Silas."

"No, I didn't. Perhaps it's time I do." He had not included the shameful truth of the kind of man he had been when first he met Jesus. His heart quaked as he looked into Diana's eyes. "There are things I must tell you." He pulled his eyes away from her, addressing everyone. "Things I have neglected to say. I've tried to forget, or atone for, perhaps. . . ." He stumbled over words. "I . . ." He kept his eyes averted from her face and from Curiatus.

"My mother died when I was very young, my father when I was twenty-two. I was an only son, and inherited all the accumulated wealth of my father and his father and his father before him. From the time I could walk, I was treated as a prince, and given every advantage money could buy: education, every comfort, position. We had houses in Jerusalem and in Caesarea. With all due respect, Epanetus, I grew up in a grander house than this, with servants to answer every whim."

He had not felt so nervous even when speaking before
the Lyconians.

"Whenever my father traveled, which was often, he took
me with him. I had an aptitude for languages and business,
and he encouraged me, giving me responsibility at a young
age." He wrung the scroll in his hands. "I was taught that
we were better than others, and believed it because of the
way we were treated wherever we went. Our wealth was
evidence of God's favor, and everyone acknowledged it.
Even Jesus' disciples thought wealth meant God's favor
until Jesus told them otherwise. It is no guarantee."

He looked around the room. *Lord, forgive me. I allowed
them to hold me in high esteem.*

Diana took the scroll from him. "I'll hold this while you
speak, lest you ruin it."

He swallowed hard. "I had heard about Jesus and the
miracles He did, and believed Him to be a prophet of
God. I wanted to meet Him. So I donned my finest robes,
mounted my best mule, called for my bodyguard and servants to see to my safety and comfort, and went out to
meet Him."

He had never felt such silence.

"I wondered at His disciples, for they were the sort of
men my father had taught me to avoid. Laborers, unedu-
cated, or at least not educated to the extent I had been."
People like these looking at him now. "One was reputed to
be a tax collector. I stayed on the outer edge of the crowd
because I did not want to brush my robe against any of
them; I thought they would make me unclean."

He shook his head, tears filling his eyes. "Such was
my pride when I went out to meet the Lord." A moment
passed before he could speak. "I was too far away to hear

everything Jesus said, and listened hardly at all. I was too busy thinking about what *I* would say and how to say it when I got close enough to Him to speak."

Silas closed his eyes. "He saw me coming toward Him and said something to the others. They made room for me to approach. I paid no attention to them. I'd been treated with that kind of respect all my life. People always made room for me."

His voice roughened. "I went up to Jesus. I called Him 'Teacher.' To honor Him, you see. Maybe even to flatter Him. And then I asked . . ." He had to swallow before he could speak. "I asked, 'What good deed must I do to have eternal life?'"

He felt a gentle touch on his foot. Diana looked up at him, her eyes filled with tears.

"Such was my pride, you see. I had given money to the poor every time I entered the Temple. I had always tithed as the Law required. One day, I would rise as a ruler among God's people. Because of wealth . . . I thought I was so *good* Jesus would have to say, 'Nothing more is required of you, Silas. The Lord is well pleased with you.' Words of praise! That's what I had heard all my life. That's what I expected, fool that I was. I wanted God's assurance before witnesses that I had a right to live forever."

He let out his breath slowly. "Jesus looked at me with such love. 'If you want to receive eternal life,' He said, 'keep the commandments.'

"'Which ones?' I asked Him, thinking one was more important than another, and Jesus listed them. 'You must not murder. You must not commit adultery. You must not steal. You must not testify falsely. Honor your father and mother. Love your neighbor as yourself.'

"I had kept all those commandments. I even thought I had kept the last one by giving a few coins to the hungry widows and orphans who sat on the steps of the Temple, the poor and destitute I graced with a paltry gift in the streets! I was so sure of myself that I said I had obeyed all the commandments and then asked what else I must do. I wanted to hear Him say, 'Nothing more.' But Jesus didn't say that."

He looked at Epanetus. "Jesus looked into my eyes and said, 'If you want to be perfect, go and sell all your possessions and give the money to the poor, and you will have treasure in heaven. *Then* come, follow Me.'

"I felt as though the breath had been punched from me. All the assurance I had lived with all my life fell away. If obedience to the Law wasn't enough, if wealth was not a sign of salvation, I was undone. I had no hope! '*Then* come,' Jesus had said. If I was willing to give up everything my father and his father and his father before him had gained, and give up all the increase I had worked to achieve, *then* I could become His disciple."

Silas gave a bleak laugh. "It was the first time my money and position had closed rather than opened a door. I went away, confused and miserable because I knew I couldn't give up anything."

"But you went back!"

"No, Curiatus. I didn't."

"But you must have!"

"I never approached Him again. Not directly. When Jesus looked at me that day, I knew He saw *inside* my heart. I was laid bare before Him. Nothing was hidden. Even the things I didn't know about myself were clear to Him. I thought it had to do with money, but He had many wealthy friends. He raised one from the grave! I didn't understand why He said all that to me, and not to others. It was a long time before I fully understood my sin.

"Money was my god. Worshipping the Lord had become mere ritual in order to retain it. 'Let go of it,' Jesus had said, 'and then you can come to Me.' And I was unwilling. I clung to what I had inherited. I continued to build upon it."

Oh, how Silas regretted the time he had wasted!

"I wanted to be able to worship God without giving up anything. So I did what I had always done. I worked. I went to the Temple. I gave my tithes and offerings. I gave generously to the poor. I read the Law and the Prophets." He clenched his fists. "And I found no peace in any of it, because I now knew that all my money would *never* be enough to save me. Jesus' words made me hunger and thirst for righteousness. I wanted to please God. I couldn't stay away from Jesus, but I couldn't face Him either."

He smiled ruefully. "Whenever Jesus came near Jerusalem or into the city, I went to hear Him. I would lose myself in the crowd or stand behind men taller and broader. I stood in shadows, thinking I was hidden from Him."

"And found you couldn't hide from God," Epanetus said.

Silas nodded. "Sometimes I talked with the disciples— never the twelve closest to him, for fear they might recognize me, but others, like Cleopas. We became good friends."

He closed his eyes. "And then Jesus was crucified."

No one moved. Silas sighed and looked around the room. The memories flooded him. "Some of my father's friends were among those who held an illegal trial in the middle of the night and condemned Him. They could not execute Jesus, so they enlisted the help of our enemies, the Romans, in order to carry out their plans. I understood them. I knew why they did it. Wealth and power! They loved the same things I did. That's what the trial was all about. Jesus was turning the world upside down. They thought when He died everything would go back to the way it was. Caiaphas and Annas, along with many of the priests and scribes, thought they could still hold everything in the palms of their hands."

He looked at his palms, and thought of Jesus' nail-scarred hands. "In truth, they held no real power at all."

"Were you at the Crucifixion?"

"Yes, Curiatus. I was there, though I wish I could have stayed away. When Cleopas and I saw that Jesus was dead, I remember being thankful it hadn't taken Him days to die."

Silas shook his head. "The disciples had all scattered the night Jesus was arrested at Gethsemane. Cleopas didn't know what to do. I let him stay with me. He went out a few days later to find the others and then came back. Jesus' body had been removed to a tomb, but now He was missing. One of the women claimed she had seen Him alive and standing in the garden outside the tomb. But this was the same woman who had had seven demons cast out of her, and I thought she had gone mad again.

"Cleopas and I were both eager to be away from the city, away from the Temple. He feared capture. I did not want to see the smug satisfaction of the scribes and priests, the Pharisees who had plotted and schemed and broken the Law to murder Jesus. Nor did I want to be around to see how the religious leaders might hunt down the disciples one by one and do to them what they had done to Jesus." His mouth tipped. "I even left my fine mule behind, and we set off for Emmaus."

Silas clasped his hands, but could not still the trembling inside. "As we walked along, we talked about Jesus. He had been a prophet; of that I had no doubt. But we were both left with so many questions.

"'I thought Jesus was the one,' Cleopas kept insisting. 'I thought He was the Messiah.' I had thought so, too, but I truly believed that had He been the Messiah, they couldn't have killed Him. God wouldn't have allowed it.

"'But the signs and wonders!' Cleopas said. 'He healed the sick! He made the blind see and the deaf hear! He raised the dead! He fed thousands of people with nothing more than a loaf of bread and a few fish! How could He do all those things if He was not anointed by God?'

"I had no answers, only questions, like he did. Cleopas was grieving. So was I. A man we didn't recognize came and joined us. 'What are you discussing so intently as you walk along?' He wanted to know. Cleopas told Him He must be the only person in Jerusalem who hadn't heard about all the things that had happened over the last few days. 'What things?' He said. Cleopas told Him, not patiently, about Jesus. We said He was a man we believed to be a prophet who did powerful miracles. He was a great teacher we thought was the Messiah, and our leading priests and religious leaders had handed him over to be condemned to death and crucified by the Romans."

Silas rubbed his hands together and wove his fingers tightly. "And then Cleopas told Him about the women who had gone to the tomb and found it empty, and Mary Magdalene, who claimed she saw Jesus alive. I'll never forget the man's words. He spoke to us as though we were frightened children, as indeed we were.

"The man sighed and called us foolish. 'You find it so

hard to believe all that the prophets wrote in the Scriptures. Wasn't it clearly predicted that the Messiah would have to suffer all these things before entering His glory?' He reminded us of prophecies we had not wanted to remember. The Messiah would be despised and rejected, a man of sorrows, acquainted with deepest grief. His people would turn their backs on Him. He would be struck, spat upon by His enemies, mocked, blasphemed, and crucified with criminals. Others would throw dice for his clothing.

"The stranger spoke the words of Isaiah I had heard, but never before understood: 'He was pierced for our rebellion, crushed for our sins. He was beaten so we could be whole. He was whipped so we could be healed. All of us, like sheep, have strayed away. We have left God's paths to follow our own. Yet the Lord laid on Him the sins of us all.'"

Silas felt the tears gather again. "I trembled as the stranger spoke, the prayer shawl over His head. I knew the truth of every word He said. My heart burned with the certainty of it. The day was late when we reached Emmaus, and we asked the man to stay. When He hesitated, Cleopas and I pleaded.

"He came in with us. We sat at the table together. The stranger broke bread and held it out to each of us. It was then I saw the palms of His hands and the scars on His wrists." Silas blinked back tears. "I looked at Him then. He drew the mantle back, and we both saw His face. For the first time since that day when He told me to go and give everything I owned to the poor, I looked into His eyes . . . and then He was gone."

"Gone? How?"

"He vanished."

Everyone whispered.

"What did you see in Jesus' eyes, Silas?" Diana spoke gently.

He looked at her. "Love. Hope. The realization of every promise I'd ever read in Scripture. I saw an opportunity to change my mind and follow Christ. I saw my only hope of salvation."

"What about all your money, the houses, the property?" Urbanus asked.

"I invested it. I sold off property as needs arose in the church. Food, a safe place to live, passage on a ship, provisions for a journey whatever was needed. I sold off the last of my family holdings when Peter asked me to come with him to Rome."

Epanetus smiled. "You gave up all of your wealth to spread the message of Christ!"

"I gained far more than I gave up. I've been welcomed to hundreds of houses, and had a home in every city I've lived in." He looked around the room, into each pair of eyes. "And brothers and sisters, fathers and mothers, even children beyond counting." He opened his hands, palms up. "And along with all those blessings, I gained the desire of my heart: the assurance of eternal life in God's presence." He laughed softly and shook his head. "I haven't a single shekel or denarius left to my name, but I am richer now by far than I was when all Judea gave deference to me as a rich young ruler."

✦   ✦   ✦

The hour was late when the gathering dispersed. Small groups left at intervals and went out different doors so they could melt back into the city without rousing suspicion. Diana and Curiatus had been among the first to go. A few lingered.

"What you've written will be read for generations to come, Silas."

Silas could only hope the copies of Paul's and Peter's letters would be protected. "The letters will guide you. . . ."

"No. I meant *your* story."

The woman turned away before Silas could say anything. He stood, a sick feeling in the pit of his stomach, as the last few disappeared into the night.

One man's view of what had happened was not a complete record of important events! All he had done was immerse himself in his memories, write his own views of what had happened. He had allowed himself to dwell on his feelings.

Silas had never walked with Jesus during those years when He preached from Galilee to Jerusalem, or traveled with Him to Samaria or Phoenicia. Silas was not an eyewitness to the miracles. He had not sat at Jesus' feet. When Jesus had told him what he must to do, he had refused!

I came late to faith, Lord. I was slow to hear, slow to see, and oh, so slow to obey!

Silas took the scroll and went into his room. *Of what value is this scroll if it leads any of Your children astray?* He added a piece of wood to the fire Macombo had built on the brazier. *Let this be my offering to You, Lord. My life. All of it. Everything I've ever done or will do. Let the smoke rising be a sweet incense to you. Set my heart aflame again, Lord. Don't let me waste my life in reverie!*

"What are you doing!" Epanetus strode across the room.

When he reached to pull the scroll out of the fire, Silas grasped his wrist. *"Leave it!"*

"You spent weeks writing the history, and now you burn it? Why?"

"They will make too much of it. And I don't want to leave anything behind that might confuse the children."

"It was all true, wasn't it? Every word you wrote!"

"Yes, as far as *I* saw it. But we serve a greater truth than my experiences or thoughts or feelings, Epanetus. The other scrolls—the ones I've copied for you—hold that truth. Paul and Peter spoke the words of Christ, and those words will remain." He released Epanetus. The scroll burned quickly now. "What I wrote there served its purpose. It's time to let it go."

Epanetus glared at him. "Are you not Jesus' disciple, too? Why shouldn't you write what you know so that it can be a record for those to come?"

"Because I was not an eyewitness to the most important events of Jesus' life. I didn't walk with Him, live with Him, eat with Him, hear every word He spoke from morning to night. I wasn't there when He walked on water, or raised a widow's son to life. Peter was."

"Paul wasn't!"

"No, but Paul was Jesus' chosen instrument to take His message to the Gentiles and to kings as well as the people of Israel. And the Lord confirmed that calling when He spoke to Ananias, and when He revealed it to me."

"Jesus called you, too, Silas. You are also a prophet of God!"

"He called me to give up that which I held dearer than God, to give it back to the One who gave it in the first place. The Lord spoke to me so that I might encourage Paul and Peter in the work He had given them. Jesus called you, too. He called Urbanus, Patrobas, Diana, Curiatus. He will call thousands of others. But what I wrote was not inspired by the Holy Spirit, my friend. It was nothing more than rambling recollections from a man in need of renewed strength. You and I and all the rest will not write anything that will stand the test of time as will words inspired by the Holy Spirit. God will use men like Paul for that, and Peter, and others."

Epanetus's face was still flushed. "The church needs its history, and you've just burned it!"

Silas gave a soft laugh. "Epanetus, my friend, I'm just a secretary. I write the words of others, and, at times, help them improve what they must say. I helped Paul because his vision was impaired. I helped Peter because he could not write Greek or Latin." He shook his head. "Only once did I write a letter, and only because I was commanded to do so. And the Holy Spirit gave me the words. Paul confirmed them."

"Believers want to hear everything that happened from the time of Jesus' birth to His ascension."

"And God will call someone to write it! But I am not a historian, Epanetus."

God knew who it would be. The Jerusalem council had discussed the matter often. Perhaps it would be Luke, the physician. He had spoken to those who knew Jesus, and he had been constantly writing notes. He had spent days with Mary, the mother of Jesus, while in Ephesus, and with John, the one Jesus treated like His younger brother. Luke had lived and traveled with Paul far longer than Silas had, and he was a learned man, dedicated to truth. Or perhaps John Mark would finish what he had set out to do the first time he had returned to Jerusalem.

Silas nodded confidently. "God will call the right man to record the facts."

Epanetus watched the scroll blacken and shrink. "All your work in ashes."

Not all. There were the letters of Paul and Peter. "It is better to burn the whole of my life than allow one word, one sentence, to mislead those who are like infants in Christ. Read the letters I'm leaving with you, Epanetus. Christ is in them. He breathed every word into Paul's ear and Peter's."

"I have no choice now."

"No. Thank God." Silas felt impelled to warn him. "You must be careful what you accept as the Word of the Lord, Epanetus. There are many who would create their own version of what happened. Just as I did with that scroll. You must measure whatever you receive against the letters I'm leaving with you. Stories can become legends, and legends myths. Do not be fooled! Jesus Christ is God the Son. He is the way, the truth, and the life. Do not depart from Him."

Epanetus frowned. "You're leaving."

"It's time."

"Where will you go?"

"North, perhaps."

"To Rome? You'll be dead in a week!"

"I don't know where God will send me, Epanetus. He hasn't told me yet. Only that I must go." He gave a soft laugh. "When a man spends so much time looking back, it's difficult to know what lies ahead."

It was late, and both were tired. They said good night to each other, heading to their chambers.

Epanetus stopped in the corridor. "Someone asked me if you ever married. If you had children. In Jerusalem, perhaps."

"I never had time."

"Were you ever so inclined?"

"Did I ever love anyone, you mean? No. Were plans ever made for me to have a wife? Yes. My father had a wife in mind for me, a girl half my age and of good family. Her father was almost as rich as mine. My father's death ended any thought of marriage in my mind. I was too busy holding the inheritance he and my ancestors had accumulated. Besides, she was very young." He smiled and shrugged. "She married and had children. She and her husband became Christians during Pentecost."

They had lost everything when the persecution began, and he had bought a house for them in Antioch. There had been times when he had wondered what his life might have been had he married her.

"You look wistful."

Silas looked up at him. "Perhaps. A little. We all thought Jesus would return in a few weeks or months. A year or two at the most."

"You miss not having a family."

"Sometimes. But I could not have done what I did if I'd had a wife and children. And I wouldn't have missed the years I spent traveling with Paul and working with Timothy."

"You traveled with Peter. He had a wife."

"We come as we're called, Epanetus. Peter had a family when Jesus called him as a disciple. I admit when I traveled with Peter and his wife, I often yearned for what they had. It was not in God's plan for me."

"There's still time."

Silas thought of Diana and heat flooded his face. He shook his head.

Epanetus gave him an enigmatic smile. "A man is never too old to marry, Silas."

"Because he *can* doesn't mean he *should*."

Epanetus nodded thoughtfully. "She would have to be a special woman, I would imagine."

"I can think of several who would make *you* a suitable wife."

Epanetus laughed. He slapped Silas on the back. "Good night, Silas."

✦   ✦   ✦

Silas awakened to Curiatus's voice in the corridor. "But I have to see him!"

"He's still asleep." Macombo spoke in a hushed voice.

"The sun is barely up." Epanetus spoke from farther away. "Why are you here so early?"

"Silas is leaving."

"How do you know that?"

"Mother told me. She said she dreamed he was on a ship and he was sailing away."

Silas heard the anguish in the boy's voice and rose from his bed. "I'm here, Curiatus. I haven't gone anywhere." *Yet.* "It was just a dream." And it had touched some chord inside him and made him tremble.

The boy came to him. "When are you going?"

He looked at Epanetus and Macombo, and down into Curiatus's distressed eyes. "Soon."

"How soon?"

"In three days," Epanetus said and looked sternly at Silas. "No sooner than that."

"I'm going with you."

Epanetus stepped forward. "Is that the way you ask—?"

Silas raised his hand. "I don't know where I'm going, Curiatus."

"You'll go where God sends you, and I want to go along!
Please, Silas, take me with you! Teach me as you and Paul
taught Timothy! Circumcise me if you have to! I want to
serve the Lord!"

Silas felt his throat tighten. The thought of going out
alone was what had held him back so long, but should
he take this boy with him? "Timothy was older than you
when he left his mother and grandmother."

"A year makes no difference."

"A year made a great deal of difference to John Mark."

"I'm old enough to know when God is calling me!"

Silas smiled ruefully. "And how can one argue with
that?" Could he take the word of a passionate boy?

Curiatus looked crestfallen. "You don't believe me."

David had been anointed as king when he was just a
boy. Silas put his hand on the boy's shoulder. "I need to
pray about it, Curiatus. I can't say one way or the other
until I know what God wants."

"He's told you to go."

"Yes, but not where."

"He sent disciples out two by two. You went with Paul.
You went with Peter. Let me go with you!"

"And what about your mother, Curiatus. Who will take
care of her?"

"Timothy had a mother. She let him go!"

There was no use arguing with the boy. "If God has
called you to come with me, Curiatus, He will confirm it
by telling me." What would Diana say about giving up her
son when she might never see him again?

Curiatus stepped closer. "I know God will tell you. I
know He will."

"Can we go back to bed now?" Epanetus spoke drily. "At least until the sun comes up?"

+   +   +

Silas fasted all day, but had no answer. He fasted a second day and prayed.

Epanetus found him sitting in the back of the garden. "Curiatus came again. Do you have an answer for him yet?"

"God's been silent on the matter."

"Maybe that means you can decide either way, though there seems no doubt in Curiatus's mind what God wants him to do."

"John Mark went out too soon."

"Timothy was younger and never looked back."

"I thought everything was settled."

"Ah yes; just pick up your pack of scrolls and walk away."

Silas cast him a dark look. Why did the Roman take such perverse pleasure in taunting him?

Epanetus grinned. "I suppose the decision is even harder when you can't have one without the other."

Silas glared at him, heart pounding. "That's the answer, then." He felt a check in his spirit, but ignored it. "If the boy isn't ready to leave his mother, I dare not take him with me."

Epanetus groaned in annoyance. "That's not what I said. And even if it was, there is a solution! You could—"

Silas stood abruptly. "I don't know where God will lead me, or whether I will ever come back this way again." He stepped past Epanetus and headed for the house. "When I leave, I will go alone." Why did he feel no relief in saying it?

"You're running scared again!" Epanetus called after him.

Silas kept walking.

Epanetus shouted this time. "Take Diana with you!"

Heat poured into Silas's face. He turned. "Lower your voice."

"Ah, that imperious tone. I've heard it often from Roman nobles. I wanted you to hear!"

"I can't take a woman! Her reputation would be ruined and my testimony meaningless!"

Epanetus snorted. "I'm not suggesting you make her your concubine. *Marry her!*"

Silas thought of Peter bound and helpless, crying out to his wife as Nero's soldiers tortured her, *"Remember the Lord! Remember the Lord!"*

Silas's throat tightened in anguish. "God forgive you for suggesting it!" His voice broke.

Epanetus's face filled with compassion. "Silas, I've seen the way you look at her, and the way she looks—"

"I'd rather kill myself now than see a woman I love tortured and martyred in front of me."

"I see," he said slowly. "But I ask you: all the while you've fasted and prayed, were you asking God what He wants you to do next, or pleading with Him to agree with what you've already decided?"

✦   ✦   ✦

When Silas told Curiatus of his decision, the boy wept. "I'm sorry." Silas could barely get the words out for the dryness of his throat. "Maybe in a few years . . ."

"You'll leave Italy and never return."

"It's best if I go alone."

"No, it isn't."

"You're not a man, Curiatus."

"I'm as much a man as Timothy was when you took him with you."

"That was different."

"How was it different?"

Silas begged God for a way to explain, but no words came. Curiatus waited, eyes pleading. Silas spread his hands, unable to say anything more.

The boy searched his face. "You just don't want me to go with you. That's it, isn't it?"

Silas couldn't look into his eyes anymore. Curiatus stood up slowly and walked away, shoulders hunched.

Silas covered his face.

Epanetus's voice rumbled low, indistinct words, but the tone was clear. He comforted the boy. Silas expected his host to come into the *triclinium* and admonish him. Instead, he was left alone.

Silas read to the gathering that evening— Peter's letters to the five provinces. Diana and Curiatus didn't come. Silas was almost thankful. He said his good-byes to the people and tried not to think about the boy and his mother. He was given a love offering to carry him on his way. His brothers and sisters wept as they laid hands on him and prayed God would bless and protect him wherever he went. He wept, too, but for reasons he did not want to think about too deeply.

"We will pray for you every day, Silas."

He knew they would keep their promise.

Early the next morning, he rose with the certainty of how he would travel, if not where. He dreamed the Lord beckoned him to a ship. He donned the new tunic Epanetus had given him. He wound the sash and tucked the pouch of denarii into it. He pinned the silver ring and knotted the leather straps that held the case containing his reed pens and knife for making corrections and cutting papyrus. Then he tied on the inkhorn. He took the coat Paul had given him and put it on, then shouldered the pack of scrolls.

Epanetus waited for him in the courtyard. "Do you have all you need for your journey?"

"Yes. Thank you. I've traveled with far less. You and the others have been more than generous."

"It has been an honor having you here, Silas."

He clasped Epanetus's arm. "An honor to me as well."

"Are you taking the road north to Rome or going down to the sea?"

"The sea."

Epanetus smiled strangely. "In that case, I'll walk with you."

They left the house and headed down the winding streets. The agora bustled with people. Urbanus gave a nod as they passed. When they came to the port, Silas looked from young man to young man.

"Are you looking for someone?" Epanetus said.

"Curiatus. I had hoped to say good-bye."

"They're over there."

Silas turned, and his heart leaped into his throat. Diana and Curiatus walked toward him, each carrying a bundle. He greeted them. "I'm glad to see you. I missed you last night."

Diana set her bundle down. "We had to make arrangements."

Arrangements?

Curiatus looked at the docks. "So which ship are we taking?"

Silas stared. "What?"

Laughing, Epanetus grasped the boy by the shoulder. "Come with me, my boy. We'll see which ship has room for extra passengers."

Silas looked from them to Diana. "He can't go with me."

"We must."

We?

She looked up at him gravely. "Silas, we prayed all night that the Lord would make it clear to us what we should do. Everyone in the church has been praying for us. You know the heart of my son. So we laid out the situation before the Lord. If you took the road north, you were to go alone. If you came to the port, we were to leave with you." She smiled, eyes glowing. "And here you are."

He struggled not to cry. "I can't take you with me, Diana. I can't."

"Because you fear harm would come to me. I know. Epanetus told me."

"You don't know."

"My body may be broken, my life taken, but I will never be harmed, Silas. Nor will Curiatus. Besides, don't the Scriptures say three together are stronger than one alone? The Lord will not give us more than we can bear, and we have heaven to receive us. And He will be with us wherever we go."

"Think how it will look to others, Diana, a man traveling with a woman. You know what people will think. How can I teach holy living if we appear to be . . ." He glanced away. "You know what I mean."

She nodded. "Living in sin?"

"Yes. So, it's settled."

Her eyes grew soft. "Yes. Of course it is. We must marry."

He blushed. "You should stay here and marry a younger man."

"Why would I want to do that when it's you I love?" She stepped close, reached up, and cupped his face. "Silas, I knew when I first saw you that I wanted to be your wife. And when Curiatus became so determined to have you take him with you, it merely served to confirm what I've come to believe: God directed your steps. The Lord brought you here, not just to rest, but to find the family He prepared for you." Her eyes glistened. "We've been waiting such a long time."

His heart pounded. "I couldn't bear to see you hurt."

"If you leave us behind, you will break our hearts."

"That's unfair!"

"Is it? It was the Lord who said a man is not meant to be alone. All these years, you've dedicated your life to helping others—Paul, Peter, Timothy, John Mark, the churches you've served. And now, God offers you a family of your own, something I know you've missed, something I know you want." She looked up, her heart in her eyes. "It is the Lord who pours down blessings upon those who love Him, Silas. You have taught that. You know it's true."

And like grace, this was a free gift he had only to receive.

"Diana . . ." He leaned down and kissed her. Her arms came around him, sliding up his back. He stepped closer and took her firmly in his arms. She fit him perfectly.

"And the Lord gave sight to the blind!" Epanetus said.

Silas drew back, but he couldn't take his eyes from Diana's face flushed with pleasure, her eyes bright with joy. He had never seen anyone more beautiful. He took her hand and smiled at Epanetus. "Indeed, He did." *And I thank You for it, Lord.*

Epanetus stood arms akimbo. "As you told me, Silas— 'You can make many plans, but the Lord's purpose will prevail.'" He winked at Diana.

The joyful sound of her laughter made Silas catch his breath. Gratitude rose up inside him like a spring of living water. She loved him! She really loved him! *I never thought to have this blessing, Lord. Never, in all my life.*

Curiatus shouted from down the quay and ran toward them. Out of breath, he reached them. He looked at Silas's hand clasping his mother's, and his face lit up. He pointed back. "There's room on that ship."

Epanetus clapped the boy on the back. "There'll be another ship, another day. First we have a wedding to arrange."

✦   ✦   ✦

The wind filled the sails, and the boat surged through the Mediterranean waters. As the bow dipped, a wave splashed up, a salty mist spraying the deck, a welcome coolness in the heat of the afternoon sun.

Silas talked to several crew members and then came to Diana. He leaned on the rail beside her. She smiled at him. "Where's Curiatus?"

"Helping one of the sailors move some cargo."

She looked out again, her expression rapt with pleasure. "I've never seen such blues and greens." She had the wonder of a child. She leaned against his shoulder. "I've never been more happy, Silas. Wherever it is we're going, I know God is the wind in the sails."

"We sail to Corsica," he said. "And then on from there to Iberia."

She glanced up at him in surprise. "Iberia?"

He saw no fear in her eyes. "Yes."

Paul had begun making plans soon after he arrived in Rome. "Peter is here," Paul had said, restless in confinement, "and so are you. We will have a church established in Rome and the work will go on. If Caesar hears my case and dismisses the charges against me, I will go to Spain. I must go, Silas! No one has gone there yet. We must reach everyone."

We.

Even under house arrest, Paul had continued the work God had given him. He had continued to dream and plan.

"We have brothers and sisters of strong faith to carry on here, Silas! But there are others who have yet to hear the Good News of Jesus Christ. Someday I will go, God willing, and if not I, the Lord will send someone else who can preach and teach. . . ."

Silas clasped his hands loosely on the rail. The sky was an expanse of blue and white.

Up there perhaps was a crowd of witnesses watching him, praying for him, cheering him on. Paul, Peter, all the friends he had known and loved.

And Jesus watched, too. *Go and make disciples of all the nations, baptizing them in the name of the Father and the Son and the Holy Spirit.*

Epanetus and the others would pray. "Yes, Lord." Spain first, and then on from there, God willing. He and Diana would keep on going as long as body and breath allowed.

Curiatus shouted, and Silas looked up. The boy climbed the mast.

Diana laughed. "He's seeing what's ahead."

When body and breath failed Silas, another would be ready to carry on.

The Word of Truth would be spoken. The Light would continue to shine.

And God would lead His flock through the gates of heaven.

DEAR READER,

You have just finished reading the story of Silas, scribe to the early church and traveling companion of Paul and Peter, as told by Francine Rivers. As always, it is Francine's desire for you, the reader, to delve into God's Word for yourself to find out the real story—to discover what God has to say to us today and to find applications that will change our lives to suit His purposes for eternity.

Though we are told little in Scripture about Silas's personal life, we do find evidence of a very committed man. He was a prominent church leader and a gifted prophet who chose to set aside what the world would view as a very promising career. He willingly became a scribe, or secretary, recording the letters of the apostles Paul and Peter.

It is interesting to note that while three of the Gospels record the story of the rich young ruler, only the Gospel of Luke refers to him as a rich religious leader. The account of the two followers of Jesus on the road to Emmaus is also found only in the Gospel of Luke. Silas was a religious leader and a travel companion of Luke. So the conjectures in this story—equating Silas with both the rich young ruler and the companion of Cleopas on the road to Emmaus—certainly aren't impossible.

Whatever the specifics of his life, we do know that Silas shed his earthly trappings of position and power in order to walk with the Lord. His life echoes that of another writer, the Author and Finisher of our faith, the Living Word, Jesus. May God bless you and help you to discover

His call on your life. May you discover a heart of obedience beating within you.

Peggy Lynch

SEEK GOD'S WORD FOR TRUTH

Read the following passage:

When they arrived in Jerusalem, Barnabas and Paul were welcomed by the whole church, including the apostles and elders. They reported everything God had done through them. But then some of the believers who belonged to the sect of the Pharisees stood up and insisted, "The Gentile converts must be circumcised and required to follow the law of Moses."

So the apostles and elders met together to resolve this issue. Peter stood and addressed them as follows: "God knows people's hearts, and he confirmed that he accepts Gentiles. He made no distinction between us and them, for he cleansed their hearts through faith. We believe that we are all saved the same way, by the undeserved grace of the Lord Jesus."

James stood and said, "My judgment is that we should not make it difficult for the Gentiles who are turning to God. Instead, we should write and tell them to abstain from eating food offered to idols, from sexual immorality, from eating the meat of strangled animals, and from consuming blood."

Then the apostles and elders together with the whole church in Jerusalem chose delegates, and they sent them to Antioch of Syria with Paul and Barnabas to report on this decision. The men chosen were two of the church leaders—Judas (also called Barsabbas) and Silas.

The messengers went at once to Antioch, where they called a general meeting of the believers and delivered the letter. And there was great joy throughout the church that day as they read this encouraging message.

Then Judas and Silas, both being prophets, spoke at length to the believers, encouraging and strengthening their faith.

After some time Paul said to Barnabas, "Let's go back and visit each city where we previously preached the word of the Lord, to see how the new believers are doing." Barnabas agreed and wanted to take along John Mark. But Paul disagreed strongly, since John Mark had deserted them in Pamphylia and had not continued with them in their work. Their disagreement was so sharp that they separated. Barnabas took John Mark with him and sailed for Cyprus. Paul chose Silas, and as he left, the believers entrusted him to the Lord's gracious care.

ACTS 15:4-9, 11, 13, 19-20, 22, 30-32, 36-40

What was the concern of the early church leaders that led to this general meeting?

Which noteworthy leaders were present?

Who was chosen to accompany Paul and Barnabas to deliver the letter? How were these two men specifically gifted?

What was their mission? How were they received?

What events took place to part Barnabas and Paul?

Whom did Paul choose as a travel companion, and where did
they go?

FIND GOD'S WAYS FOR YOU

Have you ever tried to impose restrictions on others? What
happened?

Share a time when someone imposed restrictions on you. How did
that work out?

Whom do you need to encourage and lift up? What stops you
from doing so?

STOP AND PONDER

> Let us hold tightly without wavering to the hope we affirm,
> for God can be trusted to keep his promise. Let us think
> of ways to motivate one another to acts of love and good
> works. Encourage one another, especially now that the day
> of his return is drawing near.
>
> HEBREWS 10:23-25

SEEK GOD'S WORD FOR TRUTH

In this story, the teachings of Christ disturbed Silas. Read the following words of Jesus, and see how they might be difficult for a prominent leader to hear and accept:

> Love your enemies! Pray for those who persecute you! If you love only those who love you, what reward is there for that? Even corrupt tax collectors do that much. If you are kind only to your friends, how are you different from anyone else? You are to be perfect, even as your Father in heaven is perfect.
>
> MATTHEW 5:44, 46-48

What does Jesus expect? Why?

> If any of you wants to be my follower, you must turn from your selfish ways, take up your cross, and follow me. What do you benefit if you gain the whole world but lose your own soul? Is anything worth more than your soul?
>
> MATTHEW 16:24, 26

How might Jesus' expectations have bothered Silas?

> If you love your father or mother more than you love me,
> you are not worthy of being mine; or if you love your son or
> daughter more than me, you are not worthy of being mine.
> If you cling to your life, you will lose it; but if you give up
> your life for me, you will find it.
>
> MATTHEW 10:37, 39

Why would Silas have struggled with these words of Jesus?

> Don't do your good deeds publicly, to be admired by others,
> for you will lose the reward from your Father in heaven.
> Give your gifts in private, and your Father, who sees
> everything, will reward you.
>   When you pray, don't be like the hypocrites who love to
> pray publicly on street corners and in the synagogues where
> everyone can see them. But when you pray, go away by
> yourself, shut the door behind you, and pray to your Father
> in private.
>   When you pray, don't babble on and on. Your Father
> knows exactly what you need even before you ask him!
>
> MATTHEW 6:1, 4-8

What instructions does Jesus give here? What warnings?

Who would Silas think Jesus was talking about? Why might he be bothered?

> Don't store up treasures here on earth. Wherever your treasure is, there the desires of your heart will also be. No one can serve two masters. For you will hate one and love the other; you will be devoted to one and despise the other. You cannot serve both God and money.
>
> MATTHEW 6:19, 21, 24

Again, what does Jesus expect and why?

How might these words have disturbed Silas before he chose to follow Christ?

FIND GOD'S WAYS FOR YOU

Which of these teachings seem difficult for today's culture? Which seem unfair?

What seems to be the recurring theme?

Which teaching is difficult for you personally? Why?

STOP AND PONDER

Don't let your hearts be troubled. Trust in God, and trust also in me.

JOHN 14:1

SEEK GOD'S WORD FOR TRUTH

Read the following passage:

On the day of Pentecost all the believers were meeting together in one place. Suddenly, there was a sound from heaven like the roaring of a mighty windstorm, and it filled the house where they were sitting. Then, what looked like flames or tongues of fire appeared and settled on each of them. And everyone present was filled with the Holy Spirit and began speaking in other languages, as the Holy Spirit gave them this ability.

At that time there were devout Jews from every nation living in Jerusalem. When they heard the loud noise, everyone came running, and they were bewildered to hear their own languages being spoken by the believers.

They were completely amazed. "How can this be?" they exclaimed. "These people are all from Galilee, and yet we hear them speaking in our own native languages about the wonderful things God has done!" They stood there amazed and perplexed. "What can this mean?"

But others in the crowd ridiculed them, saying, "They're just drunk, that's all!"

Then Peter stepped forward with the eleven other apostles and shouted to the crowd, "Listen carefully, all of you, fellow Jews and residents of Jerusalem! Make no mistake about this. What you see was predicted long ago by the prophet Joel:

'In the last days,' God says,
'I will pour out my Spirit upon all people.
Your sons and daughters will prophesy.
Your young men will see visions,
and your old men will dream dreams.
In those days I will pour out my Spirit
even on my servants—men and women alike—

and they will prophesy.
And I will cause wonders in the heavens above
and signs on the earth below
before that great and glorious day of the LORD arrives.
But everyone who calls on the name of the LORD will be
saved.'

"People of Israel, listen! God publicly endorsed Jesus the Nazarene by doing powerful miracles, wonders, and signs through him, as you well know. But God knew what would happen, and his prearranged plan was carried out when Jesus was betrayed. With the help of lawless Gentiles, you nailed him to a cross and killed him. But God released him from the horrors of death and raised him back to life, for death could not keep him in its grip. And we are all witnesses of this."

Peter's words pierced their hearts, and they said to him and to the other apostles, "Brothers, what should we do?"

Peter replied, "Each of you must repent of your sins and turn to God, and be baptized in the name of Jesus Christ for the forgiveness of your sins. Then you will receive the gift of the Holy Spirit. This promise is to you, and to your children, and even to the Gentiles—all who have been called by the Lord our God."

Those who believed what Peter said were baptized and added to the church that day—about 3,000 in all.

All the believers devoted themselves to the apostles' teaching, and to fellowship, and to sharing in meals (including the Lord's Supper), and to prayer.

ACTS 2:1-8, 11-14, 16-24, 32,37-39, 41-42

Discuss the prayer meeting described in this passage. Who was meeting together and why? Describe what took place.

How did the people respond?

What did Peter do?

What are some key points from Peter's message that day?

What were the results of Peter's message? Why do you think this happened?

FIND GOD'S WAYS FOR YOU
Where do you spend your time and with whom? Why?

What influence do you have on other people? What influence do they have on you?

What lasting effect will your life have? What lasting effect do you *want* it to have?

STOP AND PONDER

Don't copy the behavior and customs of this world, but let God transform you into a new person by changing the way you think. Then you will learn to know God's will for you, which is good and pleasing and perfect.

ROMANS 12:2

SEEK GOD'S WORD FOR TRUTH

Read the following passage:

Paul went first to Derbe and then to Lystra, where there was a young disciple named Timothy. His mother was a Jewish believer, but his father was a Greek. Timothy was well thought of by the believers in Lystra and Iconium, so Paul wanted him to join them on their journey.

Next Paul and Silas traveled through the area of Phrygia and Galatia, because the Holy Spirit had prevented them from preaching the word in the province of Asia at that time.

That night Paul had a vision: A man from Macedonia in northern Greece was standing there, pleading with him, "Come over to Macedonia and help us!"

We boarded a boat at Troas and sailed straight across to the island of Samothrace, and the next day we landed at Neapolis. From there we reached Philippi, a major city of that district of Macedonia and a Roman colony. And we stayed there several days.

On the Sabbath we went a little way outside the city to a riverbank, where we thought people would be meeting for prayer, and we sat down to speak with some women who had gathered there. One of them was Lydia from Thyatira, a merchant of expensive purple cloth, who worshiped God. As she listened to us, the Lord opened her heart, and she accepted what Paul was saying. She was baptized along with other members of her household, and she asked us to be her guests. "If you agree that I am a true believer in the Lord," she said, "come and stay at my home." And she urged us until we agreed.

One day as we were going down to the place of prayer, we met a demon-possessed slave girl. She was a fortune-teller who earned a lot of money for her masters. She followed

Paul and the rest of us, shouting, "These men are servants of the Most High God, and they have come to tell you how to be saved."

This went on day after day until Paul got so exasperated that he turned and said to the demon within her, "I command you in the name of Jesus Christ to come out of her." And instantly it left her.

Her masters' hopes of wealth were now shattered, so they grabbed Paul and Silas and dragged them before the authorities at the marketplace. "The whole city is in an uproar because of these Jews!" they shouted to the city officials. "They are teaching customs that are illegal for us Romans to practice."

A mob quickly formed against Paul and Silas, and the city officials ordered them stripped and beaten with wooden rods. They were severely beaten, and then they were thrown into prison. The jailer was ordered to make sure they didn't escape. So the jailer put them into the inner dungeon and clamped their feet in the stocks.

Around midnight Paul and Silas were praying and singing hymns to God, and the other prisoners were listening. Suddenly, there was a massive earthquake, and the prison was shaken to its foundations. All the doors immediately flew open, and the chains of every prisoner fell off! The jailer woke up to see the prison doors wide open. He assumed the prisoners had escaped, so he drew his sword to kill himself. But Paul shouted to him, "Stop! Don't kill yourself! We are all here!"

The jailer called for lights and ran to the dungeon and fell down trembling before Paul and Silas. Then he brought them out and asked, "Sirs, what must I do to be saved?"

They replied, "Believe in the Lord Jesus and you will be saved, along with everyone in your household." And they shared the word of the Lord with him and with all who lived in his household. Even at that hour of the night, the jailer cared for them and washed their wounds. Then he and everyone in his household were immediately baptized. He brought them into his house and set a meal before them,

and he and his entire household rejoiced because they all
believed in God.   Acts 16:1-2, 6, 9, 11-34

While in Lystra, Paul and Silas met Timothy. Discuss that encounter and the results.

Why did they travel to Phrygia and Galatia? Why did they avoid
Asia?

Describe the encounters in Philippi.

What led to Paul and Silas's imprisonment? How did they demonstrate their peace?

Discuss the earthquake and how the two missionaries responded.

What were the results of their disciplined response in the midst of mayhem?

FIND GOD'S WAYS FOR YOU

How do you handle the unexpected?

Describe a time God kept you safe.

What "chains" are keeping you imprisoned?

STOP AND PONDER

> "For I know the plans I have for you," says the LORD. "They are plans for good and not for disaster, to give you a future and a hope."   JEREMIAH 29:11

SEEK GOD'S WORD FOR TRUTH

Silas traveled with both Paul and Peter. In this story, he wrestled with the issue of celibacy versus marriage in relation to serving God. The following passages may shed some light on why this may have been a struggle for Silas.

The apostle Paul wrote:

> Now regarding the questions you asked in your letter. Yes, it is good to live a celibate life. But because there is so much sexual immorality, each man should have his own wife, and each woman should have her own husband.
>
> I say to those who aren't married and to widows—it's better to stay unmarried, just as I am. But if they can't control themselves, they should go ahead and marry. It's better to marry than to burn with lust.
>
> Each of you should continue to live in whatever situation the Lord has placed you, and remain as you were when God first called you.
>
> But let me say this, dear brothers and sisters: The time that remains is very short. So from now on, those with wives should not focus only on their marriage. Those who weep or who rejoice or who buy things should not be absorbed by their weeping or their joy or their possessions.
>
> An unmarried man can spend his time doing the Lord's work and thinking how to please him. But a married man has to think about his earthly responsibilities and how to please his wife. His interests are divided. In the same way, a woman who is no longer married or has never been married can be devoted to the Lord and holy in body and in spirit. But a married woman has to think about her earthly responsibilities and how to please her husband. I am saying this for your benefit, not to place restrictions on you. I want

you to do whatever will help you serve the Lord best, with as few distractions as possible.

1 CORINTHIANS 7:1-2, 8-9, 17, 29-30, 32-35

What did Paul have to say about marriage? about celibacy?

What reasons did Paul give for not being concerned with marriage at that time?

How might these instructions have perplexed Silas? What "stamp of approval," if any, did Paul offer?

The apostle Peter wrote:

> In the same way, you wives must accept the authority of your husbands. Then, even if some refuse to obey the Good News, your godly lives will speak to them without any words. They will be won over by observing your pure and reverent lives.
>
> Don't be concerned about the outward beauty of fancy hairstyles, expensive jewelry, or beautiful clothes. You should clothe yourselves instead with the beauty that comes from within, the unfading beauty of a gentle and quiet spirit, which is so precious to God.
>
> In the same way, you husbands must give honor to your wives. Treat your wife with understanding as you live together. She may be weaker than you are, but she is your equal partner in God's gift of new life. Treat her as you should so your prayers will not be hindered.
>
> I have written and sent this short letter to you with the help of Silas, whom I commend to you as a faithful brother. My purpose in writing is to encourage you and assure you that what you are experiencing is truly part of God's grace for you. Stand firm in this grace.

1 PETER 3:1-4, 7; 5:12

Discuss Peter's view of a godly wife

How did Peter view a wife's role? How does a husband's treatment
of his wife affect him?

What did Peter think of Silas? What encouragement did he offer?

FIND GOD'S WAYS FOR YOU
How do you view your place in life? What roles do you have in
various relationships or organizations?

How is God speaking to you about your personal relationships?
Be specific.

Do you use your position/role to promote or hinder others?
to restrict or to encourage those around you?

STOP AND PONDER

Finally, all of you should be of one mind. Sympathize with
each other. Love each other as brothers and sisters. Be
tenderhearted, and keep a humble attitude.

1 PETER 3:8

SEEK GOD'S WORD FOR TRUTH

Read the following passage:

Once a religious leader asked Jesus this question: "Good Teacher, what should I do to inherit eternal life?"

"Why do you call me good?" Jesus asked him. "Only God is truly good. But to answer your question, you know the commandments: 'You must not commit adultery. You must not murder. You must not steal. You must not testify falsely. Honor your father and mother.'"

The man replied, "I've obeyed all these commandments since I was young."

When Jesus heard his answer, he said, "There is still one thing you haven't done. Sell all your possessions and give the money to the poor, and you will have treasure in heaven. Then come, follow me."

But when the man heard this he became very sad, for he was very rich.

When Jesus saw this, he said, "How hard it is for the rich to enter the Kingdom of God! In fact, it is easier for a camel to go through the eye of a needle than for a rich person to enter the Kingdom of God!"

Those who heard this said, "Then who in the world can be saved?"

He replied, "What is impossible for people is possible with God."

Peter said, "We've left our homes to follow you."

"Yes," Jesus replied, "and I assure you that everyone who has given up house or wife or brothers or parents or children, for the sake of the Kingdom of God, will be repaid many times over in this life, and will have eternal life in the world to come."   LUKE 18:18-30

What was the first issue that Jesus pointed out to the young man? Why?

What was the second issue that Jesus wanted the young man to see? How did he respond?

What lesson was Jesus teaching His disciples? How did they respond?

What do you think Jesus meant when He said, "What is impossible for people is possible with God"?

How did Jesus answer Peter? What was in it for Peter and the other disciples?

What is the relative importance of things and people in God's economy?

FIND GOD'S WAYS FOR YOU

What "trappings" in your life need to go?

How will you respond to Jesus? When?

STOP AND PONDER

> Now may the God of peace make you holy in every way, and
> may your whole spirit and soul and body be kept blameless
> until our Lord Jesus Christ comes again. God will make this
> happen, for he who calls you is faithful.
>
> 1 THESSALONIANS 5:23-24

WHILE many of the details in this story have been fictionalized, we know that the historical Silas was a wealthy, educated, and gifted individual. He was a respected church leader and prophet. He deliberately chose to be committed to Christ—to leave behind his material possessions to become a colaborer and correspondent with Peter and Paul. Silas embraced the role of scribe, writing the words of others to promote the Kingdom of God. He chose to serve rather than to be served. He accepted God's call on his life and furthered the claims of Jesus. And in so doing, he gained an incorruptible inheritance.

Jesus was God's only Son. He left His heavenly throne, His royal priesthood and kingly comforts, to come to earth. He too chose to be committed—committed to God's eternal plan for mankind's salvation. Jesus is also a type of scribe. He writes His words on our hearts; He is the Living Word.

> In the beginning the Word already existed. The Word was with God, and the Word was God. He existed in the beginning with God. God created everything through him, and nothing was created except through him. The Word gave life to everything that was created, and his life brought light to everyone. The light shines in the darkness, and the darkness can never extinguish it. JOHN 1:1-5

Beloved, may you deliberately choose to commit yourself to Jesus and walk in His light.

FRANCINE Rivers began her literary career at the University of Nevada, Reno, where she graduated with a Bachelor of Arts degree in English and Journalism. From 1976 to 1985, she had a successful writing career in the general market and her books were highly acclaimed by readers and reviewers. Although raised in a religious home, Francine did not truly encounter Christ until later in life, when she was already a wife, mother of three, and an established romance novelist. Shortly after becoming a born-again Christian in 1986, Francine wrote *Redeeming Love* as her statement of faith. First published by Bantam Books, and then re-released by Multnomah Publishers in the mid-1990s, this retelling of the biblical story of Gomer and Hosea set during the time of the California Gold Rush is now considered by many to be a classic work of Christian fiction. *Redeeming Love* continues to be one of the Christian Booksellers Association's top-selling titles and it has held a spot on the Christian best-seller list for nearly a decade.

Since *Redeeming Love*, Francine has published numerous novels with Christian themes—all best sellers—and she has continued to win both industry acclaim and reader loyalty around the globe. Her Christian novels have been awarded or nominated for numerous awards including the Rita Award, the Christy Award, the ECPA Gold Medallion, and the Holt Medallion in Honor of Outstanding Literary Talent. In 1997, after winning her third Rita award for Inspirational Fiction, Francine was inducted into the Romance Writers' of America Hall of Fame. Francine's

novels have been translated into over twenty different languages and she enjoys best-seller status in many foreign
countries including Germany, the Netherlands, and South
Africa.

Francine and her husband Rick live in Northern California and enjoy the time spent with their three grown
children and every opportunity to spoil their four grand-
children. She uses her writing to draw closer to the Lord,
and that through her work she might worship and praise
Jesus for all He has done and is doing in her life.

BOOKS BY BELOVED AUTHOR
FRANCINE RIVERS

The Mark of the Lion Series
(available individually or boxed set)
A Voice in the Wind
An Echo in the Darkness
As Sure as the Dawn

The Atonement Child
The Scarlet Thread
The Last Sin Eater
Leota's Garden
The Shoe Box

A Lineage of Grace Series
Unveiled
Unashamed
Unshaken
Unspoken
Unafraid

And the Shofar Blew

Sons of Encouragement Series
The Priest
The Warrior
The Prince
The Prophet
The Scribe

CP0098